Dragon Claimed

Also from Donna Grant

Don't miss these other spellbinding novels!

Reaper Series
Dark Alpha's Claim
Dark Alpha's Embrace
Dark Alpha's Demand
Dark Alpha's Lover
Tall Dark Deadly Alpha Bundle
Dark Alpha's Night
Dark Alpha's Hunger

Dark King Series
Dark Heat (3 novella compilation)
Darkest Flame
Fire Rising
Burning Desire
Hot Blooded
Night's Blaze
Soul Scorched
Dragon King (novella)
Passion Ignites
Smoldering Hunger
Smoke And Fire
Dragon Fever(novella)
Firestorm
Blaze
Dragon Burn (novella)
Heat
Torched
Dragon Night
Dragonfire

Dark Warrior Series
Midnight's Master
Midnight's Lover
Midnight's Seduction
Midnight's Warrior

Midnight's Kiss
Midnight's Captive
Midnight's Temptation
Midnight's Promise
Midnight's Surrender (novella)

Dark Sword Series
Dangerous Highlander
Forbidden Highlander
Wicked Highlander
Untamed Highlander
Shadow Highlander
Darkest Highlander

Rogues of Scotland Series
The Craving
The Hunger
The Tempted
The Seduced

Chiasson Series
Wild Fever
Wild Dream
Wild Need
Wild Flame

LaRue Series
Moon Kissed
Moon Thrall
Moon Bound
Moon Struck

Shield Series
A Dark Guardian
A Kind of Magic
A Dark Seduction
A Forbidden Temptation
A Warrior's Heart

Dragon Claimed

A Dark Kings Novella

By Donna Grant

1001 Dark Nights

EVIL EYE
CONCEPTS

Dragon Claimed
A Dark Kings Novella
By Donna Grant

1001 Dark Nights
Copyright 2019 Donna Grant

ISBN: 978-1-948050-95-1

Foreword: Copyright 2014 M. J. Rose
Published by Evil Eye Concepts, Incorporated

Sign up for the 1001 Dark Nights Newsletter
and be entered to win a Tiffany Key necklace.

There's a contest every month!

Go to www.1001DarkNights.com to subscribe.

As a bonus, all subscribers can download
FIVE FREE exclusive books!

One Thousand and One Dark Nights

Once upon a time, in the future...

*I was a student fascinated with stories and learning.
I studied philosophy, poetry, history, the occult, and
the art and science of love and magic. I had a vast
library at my father's home and collected thousands
of volumes of fantastic tales.*

*I learned all about ancient races and bygone
times. About myths and legends and dreams of all
people through the millennium. And the more I read
the stronger my imagination grew until I discovered
that I was able to travel into the stories... to actually
become part of them.*

*I wish I could say that I listened to my teacher
and respected my gift, as I ought to have. If I had, I
would not be telling you this tale now.
But I was foolhardy and confused, showing off
with bravery.*

*One afternoon, curious about the myth of the
Arabian Nights, I traveled back to ancient Persia to
see for myself if it was true that every day Shahryar
(Persian: شهريار, "king") married a new virgin, and then
sent yesterday's wife to be beheaded. It was written
and I had read, that by the time he met Scheherazade,
the vizier's daughter, he'd killed one thousand
women.*

Something went wrong with my efforts. I arrived in the midst of the story and somehow exchanged places with Scheherazade — a phenomena that had never occurred before and that still to this day, I cannot explain.

Now I am trapped in that ancient past. I have taken on Scheherazade's life and the only way I can protect myself and stay alive is to do what she did to protect herself and stay alive.

Every night the King calls for me and listens as I spin tales. And when the evening ends and dawn breaks, I stop at a point that leaves him breathless and yearning for more. And so the King spares my life for one more day, so that he might hear the rest of my dark tale.

As soon as I finish a story... I begin a new one... like the one that you, dear reader, have before you now.

Prologue

1995

"Come on, Gemma!"

She heard the shout from her brother over the driving rain and crack of lightning. Gemma lifted her arm to shield her eyes from the onslaught of water while struggling to keep hold of the leash for their dog.

"Kyle!" she hollered when the animal bolted, tearing the leash from her fingers.

But the booming thunder drowned out her words.

"Gemma!"

She glanced in the direction that her dog had run. She hated storms. Her parents and Kyle knew that. Why hadn't they helped her? Anger seethed within her. They hadn't helped because they wanted to leave Daisy behind.

Well, Daisy was hers, and if she had to leave her friends and her home, she wasn't leaving her dog.

"Gemma!"

She ignored both her parents, who were now shouting her name as she raced after Daisy. If she had to carry the forty-pound dog to the boat, then that's what she'd do. Just as soon as she found Daisy.

Another flash of lightning bathed the land in light, giving her just a glimpse of the dog as she headed toward the house. Gemma ran as fast as her seven-year-old legs would carry her. She reached the house and Daisy.

"Hey, girl," she said to the terrified dog. "It's going to be all right."

It took her four tries before she was able to lift the dog. She shook badly, but at least she wasn't trying to get free. Gemma knew her parents were going to be furious with her. She didn't know why they were sneaking away in the middle of the night in a storm, but the fear in her father's voice and her mother's face let her know that the questions would have to wait.

In less than two hours, they had packed up all they could and put it on the boat her father owned. She'd asked where they were headed, but her parents hadn't answered and her brother had shot her an irritated look.

Once she got on the boat with Daisy, she hoped someone would tell her something. She hated not knowing what was going on. Kyle didn't care. He always said that their parents would tell them when they needed to know.

Gemma stumbled and fell to her knees. She pitched forward so that she had to release Daisy in order to catch herself, but she managed to keep a tight hold of the leash and pull the dog back to her. Daisy seemed to like being held, so she didn't put up a fight.

"I'm coming!" Gemma shouted, hoping her family could hear her.

She couldn't see the dock through the driving rain and dark. Which was odd. There was supposed to be a light on the dock. She knew the way to the water, so she hadn't gone the wrong way. But...why wasn't the light on?

Gemma walked faster on the incline, slipping on the wet grass. She no longer cared that the water hit her face so hard it felt like little pebbles. All she wanted was to be with her family.

"Mum! Da!" she called as she reached the wooden quay.

The waves crashed violently against the side of the isle, slapping against the rock and concrete.

"Kyle!"

Her eyes searched the area for some sign of the boat. Perhaps if she walked further out onto the dock she might see them, but some voice inside her cautioned her against going forward.

Or shouting for her family again.

Gemma stood shivering from fear and dread in the storm, her heart pounding as she realized that the boat and her family were gone. She squeezed Daisy so tight that she whimpered.

Instantly, she loosened her fingers, but she still didn't move. It wasn't just terror and shock that held her motionless. Something was out in the dark. Even though Gemma couldn't see what it was, she knew it was there.

So did Daisy. Her gaze was on it, a low rumble of a growl falling from her mouth.

Gemma didn't know how long she stood there before the alarm that had held her captive vanished. Still, she didn't move out onto the dock. The waves were becoming higher and higher as the storm intensified.

She took a step back. Then another. Gemma turned on her heel and hurried to the house. There was a window in the back that never locked. She'd use it to get inside. On her way there a flash of lightning allowed her to glimpse the outline of a person ahead of her.

A scream rose up, but Gemma held it in and veered to the right as she started running. Her attention was on the figure she'd seen, and she ended up moving too close to the edge of the isle and the mountain of boulders near. She realized her mistake the moment a wave swallowed her.

Gemma lost her hold on Daisy but managed to keep her footing. But she wasn't so lucky with the second wave. She was yanked out into the churning water. As she struggled to keep her head above water, she saw the figure suddenly standing on the boulders watching her.

She gulped in a mouthful of air before being pulled under again. With her eyes on the surface, she swam as hard as she could against the current trying to take her out into the sea. Her arms and legs grew tired and her lungs burned for air, but her fight paid off as she got free. Just as she was about to break the surface, lightning showed her that the person still stood on the edge, waiting to see if she would rise up.

Gemma stopped swimming and squeezed her eyes shut, a silent scream of terror running through her. She wanted her mum and dad. Even Kyle. Someone so she wouldn't be alone.

Her eyes snapped open. No longer could she wait. She had to get some air or drown. She pushed hard and broke the water. A quick look showed that she was now alone.

The waves pushed her closer and closer to the rocks. She barely had the energy to keep her head above water, much less fight the waves. She did manage to kick off one rock, but still scraped against several more. Gemma hissed at the saltwater that seeped into the fresh cut.

She wasn't going to survive a near drowning only to be smashed against the boulders. Gemma gritted her teeth and waited for the next wave. She used it to turn herself and push off a rock to get clear of the largest of them. Then she was able to grab the smaller ones and hang on before the wave took her back out with it.

Chilled to her bones, she clawed her way out of the water. A moment later, something licked at her face. She looked up to find Daisy. Tears stung her eyes as she rubbed her head.

"Hey, girl," she murmured.

Her arms shook when she pushed herself to her feet. Thankfully, Daisy was all too eager to go with her. It was a blessing, because Gemma didn't think she could lift her if she tried.

She made her way to the house and found the window. After she got it open, she silently and slowly climbed over the sill. It took her forever because her body wouldn't obey her properly. Once inside, she called softly for Daisy, who leapt through to land softly beside her.

Gemma shut the window against the storm and huddled in a corner behind some furniture with her dog. She wanted out of the wet clothes, but the trepidation that had held her at the water was back. Whatever had been there was now in the house. It wasn't as if she had anywhere else to go. The isle was small with only a few deserted buildings besides the house. It was a great place to play, but not somewhere she wanted to be by herself now.

Daisy trembled, wedging her way between her and the door. Gemma didn't know if the dog was cold or scared—or both. But Daisy was all she had, and she wasn't going to lose her.

She wrapped the end of Daisy's leash around her hand several times. The leash wouldn't yank out of her grasp a second time.

The storm raged for hours in the endless night. Gemma didn't close her eyes once, even when the thing in the house left. And when dawn came, she still didn't move. She remained just as she was with her behind numb, her legs stiff, and her body freezing.

Even Daisy didn't move. The dog closed her eyes, but every sound caused her ears to twitch, which was how Gemma knew the dog wasn't really asleep.

When midday came, Gemma finally rose, wincing at her stiff body. She cautiously walked through the house. Nothing had been disturbed.

She went upstairs to her room and peeled off her semi-dry clothes before finding new ones. Part of her wanted to remain there because she felt safe. But she was hungry and thirsty. And she really wanted to find her family.

Gemma took a deep breath and walked down the stairs, making sure to step around the parts of the stairs that squeaked. She went outside and stood on the back porch where she would be able to see the dock.

It was there, but there was no sign of her da's boat, or her family. Maybe they'd sailed off, waiting for the weather to calm so they could return for her.

She went back into the house and stood at the table where the dinner from the night before sat half-eaten. They'd been in the middle of it when her father had gotten a call. One look from him to her mum, and the next thing Gemma knew they were packing up.

Her stomach growled loudly. She sat and finished the food, scraping the plate clean before moving on to her brother's. Beside her, Daisy licked her lips, waiting. Gemma lowered her mother's plate to the floor to let the dog eat.

She didn't venture from the house the rest of that day. Or the three following.

By the fourth day, she went to the dock and stood on the edge, looking out at the water. That's when she knew her family had left her.

Chapter One

Present Day
Dreagan

Cináed rubbed his eyes and sat back in the chair. He should have known better than to tell Ryder he was willing to help out. Cináed thought he might get to use his skills on the computer.

Instead, Ryder had him looking through old newspapers from all over Scotland in search of anything out of the ordinary. It began three weeks ago, and Cináed made his way through one huge stack only to be told that was from Glasgow. Then he was shown other stacks.

It would help if Ryder had some idea what he wanted him to look for, but all Cináed got in reply was that if it sounded odd, put it aside.

Humans reported on every little thing. Cináed actually thought he wouldn't find many odd things in the newspaper, but he'd been wrong. More often than not, he was setting aside a paper to show Ryder.

Cináed popped the last raspberry biscuit in his mouth and reached for the next paper. He was now on the newspapers from Inverness, and finding quite a bit that was 'odd.'

He propped his foot up on the stool before him while reading about a reporter's take on the queen's recent visit to Balmoral Castle. Cináed fought to stay awake. He kept yawning as he moved from story to story with nothing catching his eye.

It was on the third page of the newspaper on the bottom right-hand side that he spotted the headline: **Young Girl Found Alone on Isle**.

Below it was a close-up picture of a pretty child with her head turned staring into the camera. The black and white photo didn't show the color of the lass's long hair that had tendrils flying across her face from the wind.

There was something in the girl's eyes that wouldn't let him look away. Misery, despair, and acceptance stared back at him from the picture.

It was several minutes before Cináed read the article about how the girl—a Gemma Atherton—was found alone. The isle had been purchased by a Mr. Ben Sinclair ten years prior. With three houses and a tiny post office, the isle only held a family of four. Presumably the girl's family.

Cináed was surprised to read that Gemma had no idea where her family had gone. The article went on to say that there was a search for the mother, father, and son across the United Kingdom, the surrounding isles, as well as the seas.

A family going missing certainly constituted something odd. Cináed put the paper aside to show Ryder later, but he soon picked it back up again. He read the article three more times. And each instance he wondered what had become of the girl and if her family had been found.

Cináed folded the newspaper so that the article was on top and picked up the rest of the oddities he'd found that day before he stood and made his way to the computer room, which was Ryder's domain.

He met Kinsey on the stairs. Ryder's mate had a box of donuts in hand as she smiled at him. He didn't need to ask if every pastry in there was jelly-filled, because those were Ryder's favorites.

"You found something," Kinsey said.

He looked into her violet eyes and shrugged. "Maybe."

"Anything you want me to look into?"

"Actually, I'd like to look myself."

Her dark brows shot up on her forehead. "I see."

They reached the door to the computer room. Cináed opened it and waited for Kinsey to enter before he followed. Ryder didn't glance away from the multiple rows of screens he watched. Instead, he held out his hand, waiting for Kinsey to take it when she walked to him. After they shared a quick kiss, she sat in the chair next to him and set the box of donuts down.

"More things for me to look into?" Ryder asked him.

Cináed set the papers on Ryder's desk but kept the top one. That got Ryder's attention. He pulled his hands away from the keyboard and focused on Cináed.

"What did you find?" Ryder asked.

Every Dragon King had their own special magic. Guy could take away someone's memories. Constantine could heal anything but death. Ulrik could bring someone back from the dead—or obliterate their soul. Kiril could freeze anything.

And the list went on and on.

For Ryder, he could make and operate anything electronic. Computers were his specialty. There wasn't a hacker in the world who could get through his firewalls. And there was no security system in operation that could keep him out.

If anyone needed anything looked for at Dreagan, they went to Ryder. With his facial recognition software, and the ability to search the entire world for a needle, he got the job done quickly.

Cináed's ability wasn't so cut and dry. When he wanted to learn something, he was able to do it. Whatever that might be. For a while he'd helped Vaughn with his legal practice, but Cináed was ready to move on to something else. He'd now turned to computers, which Ryder had been happy to show him.

Ryder slowly smiled. "Something caught your attention."

"Aye," Cináed said.

Ryder then pointed to one of the other keyboards. "Get on it."

Cináed walked to the chair. Before he reached it, Ryder had turned control of the screen to him. He sat and popped his knuckles as he glanced at the photo of the girl once more. Gemma Atherton.

What was it about that name that caused him to frown? He should know that name. Maybe he'd find out when he discovered what had happened to the child.

Cináed opened up a search page. He then typed in the girl's name and "missing family" before he hit enter. Instantly the screen was filled with links. One by one he went through them reading what was said. He highlighted anything he found important before moving onto the next.

It wasn't long before he was utterly absorbed in his search. Gemma had dominated the headlines across the UK for several months. There were many pictures of her, but in every one she had the same expression from the first photo.

Then, suddenly, there were no new pictures. The papers re-used photos. As odd as Cináed found that, what was more puzzling was that the authorities had found nothing of her parents or brother.

After a few months, Gemma's name stopped being printed as the talk centered on the missing parents and son. There was a search of the isle for bodies, which made him roll his eyes. As if Gemma had murdered her family. Anyone in their right mind could look at her and know a seven-year-old didn't do it.

Cináed frowned. This happened years ago, but he still was sure of her innocence. He finished the article and went on to the next, but there was nothing. Everything about Gemma Atherton and her family ceased.

Another search to find what had happened to Gemma netted him nothing. But Cináed had been taught by Ryder, so he wasn't deterred. His next search gave him exactly what he wanted.

Gemma had become a ward of the state and gone into foster care. He was able to bypass the security from the government and get into the files. There he discovered that Gemma's foster parents had put her into therapy to talk about what had happened, but after seven different therapists over a three-year period, everyone came to realize that she wasn't going to discuss it.

Gemma kept to herself, shying away from others. She made decent grades and finished school. As soon as she came of age, she left her foster parents' home. The documents from the government ended as well.

But Cináed knew there was more. It took some digging, and a couple of tries remembering what Ryder had taught him, but he found what he was looking for on social media using the facial recognition software.

The one final picture of Gemma in the files when she came of age made it easy to pop that into the software and search the entire Internet for her. Unfortunately, it was a search that would take hours.

Cináed pushed back the chair and ran a hand down his face. He didn't understand the connection he felt to Gemma, but it was there. Maybe he just felt sorry for her that her family disappeared.

He spun the office chair as he was about to stand, but he spotted Ryder leaned back in his own chair, legs stretched out and ankles crossed as he watched Cináed.

"You've been glued to the screen for twelve hours," Ryder said.

Cináed frowned and looked at the time. It had been twelve hours. He shrugged and swung his gaze back to Ryder. "There was a lot to look through."

"Who is Gemma Atherton?"

"I don't know."

Ryder quirked a blond brow. "She obviously intrigued you."

"I found this," Cináed said and tossed him the article. "That seven-year-old's parents and older brother disappeared one night. She wouldn't say how long she was on that isle by herself with her dog, but my guess is awhile."

"Maybe her family meant to leave her."

"Hmm. I think it's more than that. Something isna adding up."

"If I know the authorities, they took pictures of everything. Did you look at those?"

Damn. Cináed knew there had been something he was missing. He slid around as Ryder sat up and swiveled his chair to start typing. Within seconds, the pictures filled two of the many screens.

Ryder clicked on each one, letting it fill an entire screen so they could get a closer look. It didn't take long for Cináed to realize that this was no cut-and-dried case.

"Would a woman leave something that is obviously an antique behind?" Cináed asked as he pointed to the broach in one of the pictures.

Ryder shook his head. "I doona think so. No' on purpose, at least. Look at the bedrooms."

Cináed inspected each one. "They're messy. Drawers half opened. In all except this one," he said, pointing to what was obviously Gemma's room.

"I suppose the parents could have tried to get away without her knowing."

"On an isle with no one else about? And Gemma had a dog."

Ryder's lips twisted. "I forgot about the dog."

"The only way on or off the isle was by water. Is there a boat in Ben Sinclair's name?"

"Is he the father?" Ryder asked as he typed in the name.

"That's the name listed as the owner of the isle."

Ryder grunted. "That's odd."

"What is?"

"There are many Ben Sinclairs, but none of them are the one who purchased the isle."

Cináed turned to Kinsey's computer since she wasn't there and began digging into the name. Between him and Ryder, it didn't take long for them to discover that Ben Sinclair wasn't a real person. Through several shell companies, the isle was in fact purchased by a Daniel

Atherton.

"The father," Cináed said with a frown.

"There is a boat in the name of Ben Sinclair as well."

"Why did he buy both under a fake name?"

"No one does that unless they're hiding from something. Or someone."

Cináed recalled something he'd read in one of the papers. He did another hunt and found there was a storm that had hit the west coast of Scotland three weeks before Gemma was found.

"I'll be damned," Ryder mumbled. "Do you think she fell overboard and managed to get back to the isle?"

Cináed shrugged. "I've no idea, but I'd like to find out."

"Why is this important?"

"I can no' explain it," he said, meeting Ryder's hazel gaze. "I just know I have to find her."

No sooner had the words left his mouth than his computer dinged. He looked at it to discover that the search had finished.

"That was quick," Ryder said with a frown. "Too quick."

Cináed pushed his chair back to the computer and quickly ran through the photos of Gemma. There were only a few, and then nothing for several years. There were more recent ones of her going back about eight years.

"This is why you look for names as well as faces," Ryder said as he tapped his finger on the screen.

Cináed looked to discover that she had changed her name to Gemma Clacher. That was odd enough since that surname was linked to Henry and Esther North, a brother and sister who recently discovered they were adopted and their names changed to hide the fact that they were the JusticeBringer and TruthSeeker of the Druids.

"That has to be a coincidence," Cináed said.

Ryder blew out a breath. "Is it? Or does it mean something else? Look where she's living."

Cináed scanned the screen until he saw it, shock rushing through him. "She's here. Right here in the village."

Chapter Two

Some days were just so very long. And today was one of those. Gemma pushed up the blue light glasses she wore to help save her eyes from all the time spent staring at a computer screen. She yawned and shoved back her office chair as she turned to get to her feet.

As she walked around her desk she looked down at the empty dog bed. It had been two months since Buster had gotten sick and died, and while Gemma hated being without an animal, she wasn't ready to find another dog yet.

She walked into the kitchen and poured herself another cup of tea. Once she added some milk, she wrapped her hands around the mug and turned to lean on the cabinets.

The rented cottage was nice. She liked the layout, but she especially loved that she had a place to work. Usually the furnished places she found had no such space. She would either work at the kitchen table or on the couch. And she discovered she quite liked having a desk.

She brought nothing more than the few suitcases and a dog bed wherever she went. It made moving every few months easy. After so many years, Gemma really thought she would have found a place where she felt she belonged. That had yet to happen.

And she feared it never would.

There was a ding from the computer, letting her know that an email had arrived. She set her mug on the desk and opened up the email to see that more work had come through.

She preferred being on her own, which had been difficult when she needed to work. It had been by happenstance one night over a decade ago when she'd stumbled upon the advertisement. Part of her thought it might be some kind of ruse, but it turned out to not only be a real job, but it paid well.

Who knew that so many people would need online researchers? Some of her jobs were interesting, and some not so much. But it was a job that kept money in her bank account. After working for a company for a few years, she had gone out on her own. She advertised for herself and set her own prices, which meant she got to keep all the proceeds.

It wasn't exactly easy having her own business, but the challenge of it was something that she liked. Her regulars had kept her from starving until she was able to get a broader reach and bring in other clients.

Gemma read over the new job offer. She then looked at her calendar to see if she could get it done in the time allotted. The money offered was nearly twice what she asked for, but that was because the person wanted it quickly.

She added the job into her calendar, making sure to mark the due date in red, then she sent a reply stating that she would take the job once half the sum was paid up front, with the rest due when she completed the assignment.

Her attention returned to her current project, but not five minutes later her mobile phone lit up to let her know that money had been deposited into her account. To her shock, Gemma saw the entire amount, not the half that was due, had been sent.

"Well. Let's hope you become a regular, whoever you are," she said with a smile.

That was incentive enough to finish the job she was on so she could get to this new client's project. She worked for another couple of hours before she stopped to grab a quick bite to eat.

The groceries were running low. That meant she would have to get out later. The thing about living in a smaller village was that they didn't have delivery. It wasn't that she hated people. It was just that she did better on her own.

Being around so many, others running into her, the noise and smell...it was just too much. A few people she could manage, but big places made her feel as if the world were crashing down upon her.

It was why she tended to pick small villages to live in, yet she missed some of the amenities that a city gave her. Like grocery delivery.

Ah, well. Sacrifices had to be made.

She removed her glasses and set them on the desk as she rose to rinse out her empty teacup. Then she retrieved the leftovers from the night before and took them to the sofa. She got comfortable and clicked on the tele.

As usual it was a commercial. But what had her snapping up her head was when she saw that it was for a vacation to the Isle of Skye. It wasn't so much the location that caught her attention, but the fact it was an isle. She'd been thinking of her past a lot lately.

Everywhere she looked, there was mention of an isle. She'd even found a place for sale not long ago that was an unoccupied isle with a home and a few other buildings on it. It reminded her of where she had grown up.

Of where she had lost everything.

Gemma turned off the television and set aside her food since she was no longer hungry. She had to take her mind off the past before it swallowed her whole. She returned to her desk, put back on her glasses, and dove into work.

She didn't stop again until she became nauseated she was so hungry. That's when she knew she needed to eat. Though there was nothing in the house. She looked down at her yoga pants and shirt and sighed. If she was getting out, she had to make a little effort.

After she changed into jeans and a shirt, she walked past the bathroom and glimpsed her hair.

"Yikes," she murmured when she caught sight of the tangled mess.

Gemma brushed it out, but there was no helping it. With a loud sigh, she threw it up into a ponytail and turned away before she could look closer at herself.

She was out the door and walking to her car when she stepped on a pinecone. That's when she realized she had forgotten shoes. Again.

With a roll of her eyes, she turned and made her way back inside to put on shoes, only to retrace her steps once more. She could find the tiniest detail for her clients, but she couldn't remember to put on shoes.

There was no need when she never left the house. At least that's what she told herself.

She headed toward the market, but the growling of her stomach let her know that she wouldn't survive seeing all that food while waiting to eat. With no other choice, Gemma realized she was going to have to stop and eat somewhere first. There were a few places, but her favorite was The Fox and The Hound. The pub was always busy. The few times she had eaten there instead of picking up an order she found a stool at the bar away from others, and somehow, she was left alone.

The thought of hot, fresh food and a drink was too good to pass up. She swung her car around and made her way to the pub. Thankfully, the parking lot wasn't that full. Now she just had to hope that the pub wasn't either since so many walked there.

She went inside and saw the stool she favored was empty. Gemma made a beeline for it. It was set to the side of the bar almost in a corner. Anyone who sat there could be overlooked, and that was exactly what she wanted.

No sooner had her butt touched down on the stool than the owner, Laith, came over. He was nice, kind even. His gunmetal eyes caught every little thing that happened in the pub, and one look from him could quell the largest of men.

Laith's long dark blond hair was left loose today as he shot her a smile. "Is it a to-go order?"

"Not today," she told him.

His brows shot up as he smiled. "What can I get you?"

She looked over the menu and picked her food. Laith walked off before she could tell him she wanted an ale, but he returned with a pint a few minutes later.

"On the house," he told her.

Gemma was always wary of anyone who gave something away for free. "Thank you."

"You look like you could use it," he said before walking away.

She sure could. Maybe she needed to stop thinking the worst about people. But then again, that's all she'd ever known. And that could be her problem.

Her gaze looked around the pub. It wasn't packed, but there were a good number of people. A few sat on their own reading a book, doing a crossword puzzle, or just staring off into space. There were several dogs sitting quietly next to their masters' feet.

She missed Buster. Ever since her first dog, Daisy, she had never gone long without having a canine companion. Somehow she didn't feel so alone when she had a pet. Dogs loved unconditionally. They didn't care how bad she looked or if she wore the same clothes two days in a row. All a dog wanted was love and attention.

That she had in spades.

She looked longingly at the animals. Every part of her wanted to go and pet them, but that meant she would have to interact with people. Animals were so much nicer than humans.

Gemma's eyes slid away from the dogs and collided with those of an old woman sitting alone. Her gnarled fingers had difficulty lifting her glass, but she didn't ask for help. No one spoke to her, and she didn't speak to anyone. The old woman didn't hold Gemma's gaze for long either.

It was like Gemma was seeing what her future held. She was going to be that old woman sitting alone at a pub ignoring and being ignored. And she would die alone, not found until someone noticed the smell.

Bloody hell. That was a sad thought.

Maybe she should find some friends. At least one other person who might check on her so she didn't decompose in her house to be found weeks after she died.

Gemma shuddered. But she wasn't like others. She enjoyed her own company. She didn't have to be around anyone in order to feel content. She didn't need to fill her days with one engagement after the other, always surrounded by people.

All she needed was a dog and a great cup of tea.

Just like all those years ago with Daisy before she'd been found.

Those three weeks on her own had been frightening. It made her grow up a lot faster than she otherwise would have. Every night she feared whatever she'd seen would return, but it hadn't.

But to this day, she worried that it might find her again.

It was one of the reasons she'd changed her surname. That and because her name had been plastered everywhere for months. The couple who fostered her and the kids staying with them all looked at her with pity. Every kid in her school asked her if she'd killed her family and tossed their bodies into the sea to be eaten by the fish.

Everyone knew her story.

Or they thought they did. They only knew what the papers had speculated and printed.

The only one who really knew what happened was her.

And she was never going to tell anyone.

Gemma jerked when the food was set in front of her. Laith frowned slightly when she briefly met his gaze, but she threw him a forced smile to show she was fine.

But she wasn't fine. She hadn't been in so, so many years.

She was likely never to be fine again.

Gemma drank several long swallows of ale and fought the emotion that rose up to choke her when she thought of her parents and brother. When she dared—and it was only once a year, normally around

Christmas—she would think about what her life might have been like had that night not happened.

Or if she hadn't chased after Daisy.

Maybe she would be with her family now. Wherever they might be. But at least she wouldn't be alone.

Gemma lost her appetite again, but she forced herself to eat. One bite after the other until the plate was clean. She waited until Laith had his back turned, then she put the money on the bar and quietly slid off the stool. She was out the door and in her car in a flash.

Chapter Three

There she was.

It was that same haunted look in her eyes that Cináed recognized from the picture in the newspaper. She didn't throw open the pub door, but rather slipped out through the narrowest of openings.

He wanted to call her name, to have her eyes turn to him, but he didn't. She had her head down so she wouldn't have to look at anyone. He couldn't help but wonder if that's how she'd gone about life since she'd been found. No doubt she had.

And that made him sad.

He knew all about hiding. It's what the Dragon Kings had done from the moment they sent their dragons to another realm. The Kings walked alongside mortals, but they were nothing alike. Different as night and day. And while the Kings had the power and might to wipe the world of the humans, they didn't.

That was the biggest difference between the two species, because if the mortals ever found the Kings, they would stop at nothing to annihilate them.

Cináed walked toward the dark gray car as Gemma started the engine. He moved between two other vehicles so he could watch her drive past him, but she turned the other way. And when he stepped out, she backed up—slamming into him.

The hit was a small bump that did nothing other than knock him off his feet. Cináed rose up on his elbow next to the back end of the vehicle, and when he raised his gaze, he was staring into the bluest eyes he'd ever seen.

They were pale blue, like the sky in the morning. Fresh and light, new and eager for the day.

A lock of ginger hair fell against her cheek. The color was more orange than strawberry blond, but against her pale skin and blue eyes, it was stunning.

Just as she was.

The pretty child had grown into a gorgeous woman with a heart-shaped face, evocative lips, poignant eyes, and a soul that silently screamed its loneliness.

"Are you okay?" she asked, a frown marring her forehead as she squatted beside him. "You're hurt. I see the torn shirt."

Cináed glanced down at his elbow. She couldn't see the small wound that was healing as she spoke. He tucked his arm against him. "I'm fine. I wasna watching where I was going."

"No, no," she said, shaking her head. "I should have paid more attention. I'm so sorry. I was lost in my thoughts, and I nearly killed you."

"It was no' near so bad as that." He gave her a smile.

And to his delight, some of her concern faded.

Cináed climbed to his feet and dusted himself off. "See? Nothing more than a ruined shirt. I think I got off pretty good considering this was my fault."

The frown was back as she studied him while straightening. "The blame lies with me. It seems I'm fortunate that I didn't do more harm. I feel as if I need to take you to the clinic to get looked over. What if you hit your head?"

He spotted Laith and Iona at the door of the pub and prayed that neither said anything. Cináed lifted one shoulder in a shrug. "I've got a verra hard head. Just ask any of my friends."

She glanced inside the car, as if wanting to get away. Indecision marred her face before she sighed. "Wait a moment."

His eyes raked down her slim form encased in jeans and a plaid long-sleeved shirt with sleeves she had rolled to her elbows. She was thin, almost too thin, like she had missed some meals, but there was no denying her curves.

She returned a moment later and held out a piece of paper. "This is my information in case you find that you are hurt more than you think. Please let me know so I can pay the bill."

He looked down at the paper before catching her gaze. "Gemma."

"That's me," she said with a nervous laugh.

Not to miss an opportunity, Cináed reached into his back pocket and used his magic to produce a business card with his name and mobile number to hand to her.

She took it, her brows snapping together when she spied the double dragon head logo that represented Dreagan scotch. "You work for Dreagan?"

"Something like that," he replied.

Her gaze lowered to the card, and when she paused, he knew she was looking at his name. Few knew how to pronounce it when seeing it written.

"It's pronounced Kinnay," he told her.

A true laugh fell from her lips and went straight to his balls. Cináed had to fist his hands not to reach out and touch her.

"Of course. I should know that. It's been awhile since I've seen such a name."

"And where did you see names like that before, lass?" he asked, not wanting to let such an opportunity pass.

She shrugged half-heartedly. "On the isles. Were you teased mercilessly as a child?"

"No' too badly."

Her lips turned up in a smile. "That's good then." She cleared her throat then. "I'm sorry I ran into you."

"It was nice to meet you, Gemma."

She hesitated a moment and nodded. "It was nice to meet you, too."

But Cináed wasn't so sure she meant it. It was there in the way she quickly looked away. She had put up walls around herself so long ago, and she reinforced them often, making sure that no one could get in.

He watched her climb into her car and drive away. It wasn't until she was out of sight that Laith walked over to stand beside him.

"You actually let yourself get hit?" Laith asked in disbelief.

Cináed cut him a look. "I didna think she was backing up this way."

"Mm, hmm. Right. So what is really going on? What's your interest in her, because there is obvious interest?"

"I'm no' sure yet."

Laith slapped him on the back. "Good luck with whatever is going on."

Cináed nodded as Laith walked away, but he wasn't really paying attention. All he saw in his mind were perfect blue eyes. "What happened to you on that isle, Gemma?"

Perhaps it was time he took a closer look. Cináed hurriedly got into the Range Rover and sped back to Dreagan. One of his most recent endeavors was learning to pilot the helicopters so he didn't have to count on Lily or Denae to fly him.

While he liked the ability to do it on his own, it frustrated him that he couldn't fly there as a dragon. In short order, he was in the luxury helicopter and starting the engine.

His head jerked around when the passenger door opened and Merrill climbed in. Cináed rolled his eyes when he saw the wide smile of his friend. He should've known that he wouldn't get to leave Dreagan on his own.

Merrill put on the headphones, his grin never fading. "I hear you have an interesting trip planned. You didna think to go without me, did you?"

"Of course no'," Cináed replied.

"Just what I thought."

"Who told you?"

Merrill shrugged and looked out the front. "Does it matter?"

Since there was very little that was kept secret at Dreagan, it didn't. And perhaps it was a good thing that he wasn't going alone. Merrill was another set of eyes that would help him uncover any clues.

Cináed began to take off. As he did, his gaze went to the manor, and at the back he saw the unmistakable wavy blond hair of the King of Dragon Kings. Constantine gave a bow of his head, an acknowledgement that he knew what Cináed was up to and approved.

"It willna be long now," Merrill said.

He looked over into his friend's dark blue eyes and nodded. There was no need to ask. Everyone knew that tensions were at a breaking point with Usaeil. Especially since they recently discovered that the Queen of the Light Fae was also part of the Others.

Just the thought of the Kings' new foe made anger churn in Cináed. The Dragon Kings' magic was mightier than any other being on the realm, but somehow the Light and Dark Fae and *mie* and *drough* Druids had joined their magic together. That combination proved to be lethal to the Dragon Kings.

Cináed didn't want to think about them right now. He'd much rather concentrate on Gemma and her untold story.

"I saw what you and Ryder found," Merrill stated. The King of the Oranges had always been direct.

Cináed glanced at him as he flew east toward the small isle where Gemma had been raised. It was part of the Hebrides Islands, and with so many of them dotting the waters, it was amazing that she had been found at all.

"I also heard you met her."

Cináed sighed loudly. "Nothing stays private."

"You let her run you over. How did you think that wouldna make the rounds?" Merrill asked with a laugh.

Cináed found himself chuckling as well. "I didna mean to get hit. It just happened. However, it did give me a chance to talk to her."

"And?"

"She's going to be a tough nut to crack."

Merrill crossed his arms over his chest. "Why do you want to know her story so badly?"

"I can no' say. I just have to."

"And her taking the name Clacher gave you the excuse you needed."

Damn Merrill. He shot his friend a flat look.

Merrill threw up his hands. "I'm on your side. Why else do you think I'm here?"

"To see if I do something else stupid."

"Well, there is that."

Cináed shook his head. "Despite Ryder's attempts, he's found no sign of her family. They disappeared that night."

"No one disappears," Merrill stated, his voice solemn.

"No, they doona."

Cináed looked to Merrill to find his friend's head of short dirty blond hair was turned to stare out the side. The smile was gone. No doubt Merrill was thinking of when they'd sent their dragons away.

"If Ryder can no' find the family, then they're gone," Merrill said.

"You mean dead."

Merrill swiveled his head to him. "Aye."

"Why leave the daughter alive?"

"They didna want to kill a child."

Cináed shook his head. "Gemma had an older brother. Kyle is gone along with the parents."

"We'll find some answers soon."

Cináed saw the red light on the map flashing, indicating that he was drawing close to the coordinates that he had entered.

When they reached the isle, he flew them over it first one way, and then the other to get a look at the land, but also to see if either of them felt any spells that would alert someone to their presence. Luckily, they felt no magic.

It was a small isle, but there were places a child could run and play. The buildings were in ruin now, with part of the main house's roof caved and parts of every building missing.

He landed the chopper and shut off the engine before they removed their headsets and exited. The first thing Cináed noticed when the helicopter blades stopped was the whistle of wind.

"There are many caves beneath these isles," Merrill said, his gaze directed toward the water.

He jerked his chin to the sea. "Go."

It was a long moment before Merrill said, "Later."

They each went a different direction. Cináed walked to the house. It didn't take long to go through each room because there was nothing to discover. The other buildings didn't yield anything either. He made his way to the dock. As he stood on the edge watching the waves break in the distance he imagined how it would have been that night with the storm raging.

The reports spoke of violent lightning and gale winds. Surely the parents would have secured the children in the boat themselves. At least that's what he would've done. If Gemma had been his child, nothing short of death would have stopped him from getting to her.

But if the boat had wrecked, there would have been proof of that. There had been no sign of the boat or bodies ever discovered. The only way anyone knew that something terrible happened was when Gemma had been found.

Merrill came up beside him then.

"The answers are in the water," Cináed said.

Without a word Merrill dove into the water, shifting into his true form as he did. Cináed was right behind him. The moment his body was beneath the waves, he released his dragon.

Merrill swam ahead of him. While he might be a dragon, Merrill's domain had been the water, specifically these waters. No one knew them better.

If there were something to be found, his friend would discover it. But Cináed had a feeling that it would give very few answers when they did. Instead, bringing forth more questions.

Chapter Four

"Gemma!"

She bolted upright in bed at the sound of her brother's voice ringing in her head. The flash of lightning, followed almost immediately by the boom of thunder had her scrambling out of bed. Except her feet got tangled in the sheets and she fell hard to the floor. Gemma didn't care that she banged her head during the fall as she crawled her way into the corner and drew her legs up to her chest.

With no dog to hold on to, she had to deal with the paralyzing terror on her own. And to make matters worse, flashes of that long-ago night went through her mind each time the lightning lit up the sky.

Finally, she squeezed her eyes shut, not that it did any good. Her heart slammed against her ribs, her breathing was harsh and ragged, and sweat ran down the sides of her face.

"It's just a storm. It's just a storm," she tried to tell herself.

But there was something about the severity of it that took her back to the fateful night her life was forever changed. A night that she tried her hardest never to think about—but the memories were always there, waiting to rise up at the worst times.

She knew in her heart that her family was dead. They wouldn't have left her behind. They loved her.

If only she could know if it was the storm that had taken them. Or if it was the figure she'd glimpsed.

Even now after so many years the thought of that tall, black silhouette in the storm made her shiver in dread. It had watched her, as if waiting to see if she would die. It was what had been on the docks, and she knew it had been in the house.

Who was it?

The better question should be *what* was it?

And why had it come to the isle?

"Mum," Gemma whispered as the tears fell from her eyes and down her cheeks.

She hadn't cried for her family in years, but today she keenly felt their absence. And the pain went so deep that it took her breath away.

Gemma didn't move the rest of the night even when the storm finally passed, leaving nothing but the steady pounding of rain. She watched the sunlight stretch through the blinds on her window across the floor.

She didn't know what time it was when she made herself climb to her feet. Every inch of her body hurt. She would be sore from holding herself so tense.

Gemma changed into a pair of sweats and an old tee shirt that she had cut the neck out of so it hung over one shoulder. She ran her fingers through her hair, put on a pair of socks since her feet always got cold, and went to put the kettle on for tea.

While the water heated, she went to her desk to look at her planner and see what she had on her schedule. Besides a conference call at one o'clock with one of several private investigators she used, her day was quiet.

Since she'd made sure to get enough groceries to last her nearly a week, she didn't have to go out at all. Unless she wanted to.

And she never wanted to.

Then her thoughts went back to the incident at the pub. She still couldn't believe she had backed into someone. And not just any someone. Cináed was so gorgeous that she had forgotten how to talk for a moment.

The first thing she'd noticed was how casually he sat on the ground, as if he got run over every day. Cináed had worn a form-fitting beige shirt that showed off his incredible physique. He was just as she liked them. Toned and defined without looking overly so.

The shrill call of the kettle had her rising to her feet to go to the kitchen. While she made her tea she thought of Cináed's face. And what a face it was.

All hard lines and ruggedness that would make the stoutest of hearts weak in the knees. His gray eyes had never wavered from hers. They had been clear and direct, penetrating even. His hair was perfect with it being extra short on the sides and back but elongated on top and worn back-swept like a pompadour without a strand out of place.

Some might say his hair was pale brown. She saw dozens of colors. Rich browns like the earth after a fresh rain, then softer shades of amber and whisky all mixed in with golden strands that reflected the sun.

One look at him, and she'd been awestruck. Utterly. Completely.

Then he spoke. The sound of his slightly roughened, sexy voice had actually made her stomach flutter. Until she realized she had backed into him. Her embarrassment made it nearly impossible for her to look at him.

But someone as handsome as he was couldn't be ignored. She had looked as much as she dared while drowning in humiliation. It had been the right thing to do to give him her information in case he was injured, but a part of her wished she could give it to him under different circumstances.

But who was she kidding? Relationships and her didn't mix. No one understood her need to be on her own when the memories of the past hit, when she evaded questions about her family, or when she wouldn't talk of her past.

The one time she had told a man who she really was, it had backfired on her. Instead of making him understand her better, she became a sideshow he could tell anyone he knew about. That was the one and only time she had dared such a thing.

No, she was much better off on her own.

She made her way back to her desk, her gaze catching on the dog bed. Maybe it was time to get a new companion. She always went to the older dogs, the ones who had been abandoned. The sadness in their eyes was one she recognized well.

Gemma loved giving the dogs a home and love. Unfortunately, it meant that she lost them more quickly than she liked. Still, it made her heart feel good to turn to the animals that no one wanted. She loved puppies like anyone else, but no animal deserved to be set aside simply because they were aging or sick.

Her work schedule allowed her to be with the dogs at all times, tending to them when it was needed, and showering them with all the love she had. And she had so much to give.

She sat at her desk and turned to the small file cabinet. After tugging the drawer open, she fingered through the files when she saw the one she had stuffed into the back. It was full of every bit of information she had researched for three years about her family.

Every newspaper clipping, every article was in there. She kept each and every tiny nugget of a lead, but every single one led her to one dead end after another.

All these years she had hoped that her family was somewhere else with a different name, happy and alive. She wouldn't have been pleased to learn she'd been left behind, but at least they would be alive.

She couldn't get even that.

It was as if someone had set out to destroy her. Why then hadn't they finished her off? Why had they let her live? Maybe they were waiting. If that was the case, she wished they'd just get on with it.

Gemma shut the drawer and turned to the computer. Instead of getting back to her work, she found herself looking at the business card that Cináed had given her. When she returned home she'd set it on her desk.

Unable to resist, she did a search on Dreagan. The first pages that popped up were things she already knew. The distillery was only a few miles from her, and it was the highest-rated, bestselling scotch in the world.

And Cináed worked for them. She shouldn't be shocked by that with the distillery being so near along with the constant flow of tourists coming through for a tour. Somehow, it did surprise her.

Her quick search soon turned into all-out research on Dreagan. The majority of companies had what they wanted the world to see, but if someone dug deep enough there were secrets, scandals, and interviews that they wanted kept buried.

It didn't matter how deep Gemma looked, there wasn't a single shred of dirt on Dreagan. The closest she got was to the now deleted video about dragons. She had seen the video when it first went live and she was living in Edinburgh. How anyone could believe that was real boggled her mind.

She'd believed it was a publicity stunt, but now that the video was gone—meaning there wasn't a single screenshot of it anywhere—made her rethink things. It could have been something by a competitor and Dreagan had it removed. Quietly, of course.

Yet she wasn't satisfied. Every company—every single one—had something they wanted kept hidden. Dreagan had something as well, but they were just better at burying it than others. She really wanted to meet whoever did their work, because it was impressive.

She was good at her job, unearthing all sorts of things as she did her research. And yet, she was stumped. This time.

Gemma moved on to Cináed himself. She typed in his first name but hesitated when she saw his last name was Dreagan.

"Bloody hell," she murmured.

Of course she hadn't been paying attention yesterday and literally ran over a guy too gorgeous for words only to find out he was part of a multi-billion dollar business. It would be just her luck that they sued her.

She moaned in remorse and lowered her head to her desk, thumping it softly.

Her head snapped up when there was a knock on her door. Gemma frowned. She hadn't ordered anything, so she wasn't expecting anyone. And no one ever came to her door. There was a part of her that wanted to act like she wasn't at home. She'd done it plenty of times, but today she rose from her chair and walked to the door.

She had to rise up on her toes to look out of the peep hole. All she saw was the back of a head. Then he turned around.

Gemma gasped and jerked back at the sight of Cináed. She hadn't actually expected him to come to her house. How the hell had he found her? She'd only given him her email.

Then again, it was a small village. And with his resources, no doubt he was able to discover where she lived rather quickly.

She put one hand on the doorknob and the other on the deadbolt. Inside her a war raged over whether to find out what Cináed wanted or to remain silent. If he wanted to sue her surely he wouldn't come to her himself. Right? At least that's the chance she was taking when she turned the deadbolt.

Gemma cracked open the door a few inches. Cináed smiled as soon as he saw her. She couldn't help but return it. There was something about him that drew her to him, something inexplicable that she couldn't quite name.

All she knew was that the world was a little brighter when he was near. And she liked it.

Chapter Five

The moment Cináed saw Gemma, he had his breath taken away. Again. He wished he could explain what it was that pulled him toward her. He'd thought it was her story and the photo of her after she'd been found on the isle that stayed with him, touching him.

But he wasn't so sure anymore.

He was beginning to believe that it might be something to do with Gemma herself. And he wanted to find out everything about her.

"Hi."

She swallowed, her blue eyes staring at him. "Hello."

Cináed feared he might have woken her. "I can come back. I didna mean to wake you."

"You didn't." She reached up and touched her hair. "I work from home, so I don't dress up."

"If I was able to work from my house, I wouldna dress either." He ended it with a smile, trying to get another from her.

Because every time he saw her smile, it made his knees go weak.

Gemma's gaze briefly dropped to the ground then she stepped aside, opening the door wider. "Would you like to come in?"

"Only if I'm no' disturbing you."

"I work all hours, so it's fine."

He stepped over the threshold into the small cottage. It was homey, but neat. Nothing was out of place. There were few furnishings, but with his digging, Cináed learned that she had rented the place furnished. "It's verra nice."

She closed the door behind him and shrugged. "It's a rental, but I like it. It's the office space that sold me."

"So what do you do that allows you to stay at home?" He already knew, but it was the question anyone would expect him to ask.

Gemma moved past him to the kitchen, where she reached for a mug and raised her brows in question. Cináed nodded. "I'm a researcher. I worked for a larger company for several years, but then I went out on my own. I have all sorts of clients. Some are companies, some are writers wanting information for a book, and I have the odd individual here and there."

"Yes, please," he said when she raised up the milk for his tea. "That sounds nice. What exactly do you research?"

"Anything and everything. I do a lot on my own, but there are times I have to hire a private investigator."

"To follow someone?"

She laughed, the sound going straight to his cock. He loved that her hair was mussed from sleep. And he thought her thick red socks were adorable.

"The PIs are pretty handy for a lot of things," she explained. "For the most part, I can do ninety-seven percent of the work myself from the computer and phone, but sometimes I need people on the ground. If I'm near a city, I do it myself. Other times it's easier to call one of the PIs. I use them because they're trustworthy, and they don't ask too many questions."

"Makes sense. Thank you," he said when she handed him the tea. He took a drink and smiled to let her know he liked it.

Gemma took a deep breath and met his gaze. "Are you hurt? Is that why you've come?"

Cináed should have expected her to ask that. He gave a shake of his head and walked to the counter where he set the cup down. "I came to let you know that I'm perfectly fine."

"I backed into you hard enough to knock you on the ground," she said. "I also saw your ripped shirt, and I was sure I saw blood."

"I doona have a scratch on me. I assure you. I knew you'd be worried. That's why I came."

She studied him a moment, her gaze narrowing as her lips twisted. "You're a Dreagan."

He shrugged. None of the Kings had last names, so when one was needed, they used Dreagan. "So?"

"Well...I don't know. I guess I thought you might seek compensation or something."

"Gemma, I was as much as fault as you were. I didna get out of the way. If anything, you could sue me."

Her eyes grew large as she took a step back. "I would never."

"Please believe me that I'm no' at all harmed from yesterday."

She nodded reluctantly. "Thank you for that."

He saw the dog bed before her desk and glanced around for the animal.

"Buster died a few months ago," she explained. "I'll get another dog soon, but I'm not quite ready."

"We have a few dogs at Dreagan. Two herders for the sheep and cattle, but we also have a Great Dane."

Her lips curved into a heart-stopping smile. "Really? I love Great Danes. Actually, I love all animals."

"You're welcome to come see Duke and the others."

"I-"

"It's the least you could do after running into me," he said before she could refuse.

She cut him a look. "Oh, I see what you're doing."

"You love animals. We have three dogs, several cats, and too many sheep and cattle to even count. Why no' come see it all?"

"Why?" she asked warily.

Cináed shrugged. "Maybe I like you."

"People don't usually like me."

"They doona see you."

She tilted her head to the side, her ginger hair falling over her shoulder. "And you do?"

"I do."

"And what do you see?" she asked in a soft voice.

Cináed took a breath and released it. "I see someone who shies away from the world. I see a woman who has a beautiful smile and a big heart. I also see someone who has suffered. It's in your eyes. Some might believe it's a mask of indifference, but you just want to hide your pain."

She was silent for a full minute. Then she said, "How do you know this?"

"I recognize it because I too have much pain to hide."

Gemma looked away.

Cináed knew he'd gone too far. He hadn't meant to say all of that, but it had been out of his mouth before he could stop it. There was so much he wanted to tell her, but now wasn't the time. He wasn't sure there was a time for it.

And there was a chance that she wouldn't react well to what he had discovered.

"You know, don't you?" Her gaze slid back to him. "You know about my past. You know who I am."

"Aye." He wasn't going to lie to her. That was the last thing she needed.

She shook her head, rolling her eyes. "Of course. You looked into me after yesterday. I should have known you'd do that."

When she turned and began gathering files, Cináed quickly walked to her. "What are you doing?"

"It's time for me to leave."

He put his hand atop hers, stilling her instantly. He waited until her gaze lifted to his. "I doona want to exploit you in any way. If you want to know, I'll tell you how I discovered you."

Cináed paused, wondering how far he should go. Then he realized it was all or nothing. This might be his only chance with her. "And if you want, I'll tell you what I found when I did a search for your family."

"What?" She jerked her hand from his, glaring at him as if he was the devil himself. "You're actually going to use that? You want to play on my emotions."

"No," he assured her. "I want to help."

Gemma snorted loudly. "You think I haven't used everything at my disposal? It's what I do for a bloody living!"

Damn. This wasn't going at all as he'd hoped. Cináed took a step back so she wouldn't feel as if he were crowding her. "I've no doubt you've done a thorough job. However, there are... things...I'm able to get done."

"Because of your money," she said with a sneer.

"Something like that."

Cináed had messed up, and badly. Merrill had suggested that Cináed get close to Gemma and then tell her what he knew. But he hadn't wanted to do that. That seemed like trickery, and he wanted honesty. She deserved that.

Or at least as much honesty as he could give her.

He reached into his pants pocket and drew out the locket. "My friend, Merrill, and I went diving off the isle near the dock. It took some time, but we found this." Cináed set the jewelry on the desk. "I believe that belonged to your mother."

Gemma never took her eyes from his face.

"If you want my help, you have it," Cináed told her. "Come to Dreagan and ask for me any time. But please doona leave the village on my account. You will never see me again, and no one from Dreagan will bother you. You have my word."

He thought she might say something, but she remained silent. Defeated, he turned on his heel and walked to the door. When he reached it, he paused and looked over his shoulder for one more glimpse of her. Then he walked out.

As he made his way to the Range Rover, Cináed wondered if she would stay. Even if she didn't, he wasn't going to stop looking into what happened to her family. It wasn't an accident, of that he was sure.

The little time he and Merrill had spent on the isle proved that. Actually, it was what wasn't in the water that raised their suspicions. There was plenty of debris from boats, but all was much older than what they were looking for.

They widened their search, picking up anything that resembled wood or parts of a boat, but nothing matched the one that belonged to the Atherton family.

It was Merrill who found the necklace. Once it was cleaned they saw the initials on the back. They matched those of Laura Atherton's. Ryder was then able to find a photo of the mother wearing the locket.

There was a chance that the necklace had been lost before that night, but there was also a good chance that it had fallen into the water the night they disappeared. Cináed hoped Gemma might be able to tell him.

He really wished he knew why finding out the truth to her story was so important. All he knew was that it occupied his thoughts and drove him to keep searching, keep looking for answers. For her.

For himself.

He drove back to Dreagan wondering how he could rectify what he'd so badly ruined. His search into Gemma proved that she moved constantly. It was his visit today that would have her leaving sooner than she'd planned.

When he returned to the manor, Merrill was waiting for him.

"Well?" his friend asked when Cináed climbed out of the SUV.

He shook his head. "It didna go well."

"Just as I knew it wouldna. What are you going to do?"

"Keep looking into that night. The answers are there. I feel it."

Merrill shrugged nonchalantly. "Then we go back. We keep looking. What are you going to do if we do find answers?"

"I'm going to give them to Gemma."

"Yourself?"

Cináed shot him a dry look. "She doesna want to have anything to do with me now. I'll send her whatever we find." He wrinkled his face. "I really thought being upfront and honest was the way to go."

"She's too closed off," Merrill pointed out. "You noticed that from the beginning. Those like that doona welcome anything that disrupts their world, and you did just that. She's been on her own for so long. I'm no' sure if it's that she doesna trust people or that she just doesna know how."

Cináed ran a hand down his face. "It doesna matter now, I suppose."

"You wanted to get to know her."

Cináed had the denial on his lips, but he didn't say it. Instead he looked into Merrill's blue eyes. "Aye. I really did. There was something about her."

"Then doona let her go."

"She's no' someone who can be held," Cináed said, though he really wished it were otherwise.

Chapter Six

He'd looked into her family. Gemma shouldn't be surprised, and yet she was. She was flabbergasted actually. After all the precautions that she'd taken through the years, somehow Cináed had discovered who she was.

That's what rattled her the most. She wanted to know how.

"No, dammit," she said to herself. "I don't."

But she knew it for the lie that it was.

Her gaze moved to the locket on the table. Emotion welled up inside her, choking her. Tears rolled down her face as she was transported back to that night years earlier.

"Hurry, Gemma," her mother said over the storm.

Gemma yanked back on her mother's arm. "I don't want to leave my stuff."

"It's just toys. We can buy you new things."

"I like my dolls."

"Laura!" her dad yelled from downstairs.

Her mother knelt before her and pulled the locket from underneath her shirt. "Come with me right now and I'll let you wear this."

For as long as Gemma could remember she'd wanted to wear the locket. The fact her mother never took it off only made her want it even more.

"Really?" she asked hesitantly, wondering if she could really get that lucky.

Her mother smiled brightly. "It'll be yours from now on. But you have to come with me now."

Gemma immediately took her hand. They rushed down the stairs, her toys and dolls forgotten. It wasn't until they were at the boat that she called out to her brother.

Kyle stuck his red head out of the hull. The hood of his rain jacket did little to keep his hair dry. "What?"

"You have Daisy, aye?"

There was a pause as Kyle looked to their father. Gemma felt her mother's hands grab her, getting ready to lift her over the side of the boat. That's when Gemma knew the dog wasn't with them.

Then she heard Daisy's bark.

She jerked out of her mother's arms. "I'm not leaving Daisy!"

"Gemma, we have to leave. Now!" her father bellowed.

She always listened to her parents, but she had to bring Daisy. Gemma hastily took several steps back while her mother reached around to the back of her neck.

"Look, Gemma," her mother said as she held out the locket. "It's yours now. Come and get it."

Gemma wanted it badly, and she was going to have it. Just as soon as she got her dog. She spun on her heel and raced back to the house for Daisy. The last thing she heard was her brother screaming her name.

She gasped, her eyes squeezed closed as the memory faded. Gemma's knees gave out and she collapsed onto the floor. A bellow of regret, grief, and sorrow filled the tiny cottage. She curled inward, her forehead against the floor as she cried.

The past could be a cruel bitch, bringing into focus minute details that she had forgotten before. The mention of the locket would have been enough to knock her on her arse, but actually seeing it? That had been like a sucker punch to her stomach.

She rolled onto her side and kept her legs tucked against her. Dried tears stained her face. She sniffed, wishing she had a tissue and decided to use the sleeve of her shirt.

Her mind wandered in various directions, but it all came back to the locket—and the fact that Cináed had found it. He'd offered to give her answers.

What made him think he could find things that she had spent most of her life looking for? She was good at her job. She hired people who were good at their jobs. Yet neither she nor anyone else had found the locket. Had Cináed just gotten that lucky?

Or was he that good?

Perhaps it was time she found out. Why let her pride get in the way of gaining the answers she longed for? Because that's exactly what it was. Her bloody pride.

Gemma pushed herself into a sitting position with her hand and wiped her face. She forgot about the work she was supposed to be doing as she rose to her feet and found some shoes. After grabbing her purse and keys, she was out of the house and inside her car in the next few minutes.

It wasn't until she was pulling into Dreagan that she realized she hadn't changed. She glanced down at herself and winced. Not exactly giving a good impression.

"Why do I care?" she asked aloud. "There's no one here I want to impress."

Then she recalled Cináed's gray eyes. They looked at her as if she were the only person in the entire world. As if he saw *her*. All of her. The good and the bad. The broken parts and the determined bits.

It was as if he noticed all the pieces that made her unfit for others and accepted her.

Or maybe she had been on her own for so long that she was seeing things that weren't there. That had to be it. To think differently was setting herself up for pain that she didn't want or need.

Ever.

She parked and shut off the engine. Gemma let her gaze wander over the parking lot that was filled with vehicles. She spotted a large group being led by someone from one of the buildings. Obviously a tour group.

People came and went from another building. Gemma leaned her head to the side and read Gift Shop. Since she didn't see anywhere else to go and ask for Cináed, she decided that was as good a place as any.

She briefly debated going home and changing, then resolve took her. She didn't care how much money those at Dreagan had. She didn't care that Cináed was so gorgeous that he outshone the sun. So what if she looked bedraggled and had on clothes most wouldn't even wear around the house? This was who she was. They could take it or leave it.

Just as soon as they gave her the information she needed.

She climbed out of her car and shut the door behind her. Then, with her chin raised, she walked to the door of the gift shop. As soon as she walked in, she was surrounded by all things Dreagan. Mostly whisky—in so many different bottles and styles that her eyes nearly crossed—along with attire, coasters, glasses, and anything else people would buy with the logo.

A part of her wanted to walk through the shop and see what all there was. Especially when she caught sight of a sweatshirt that looked so comfortable she might never take it off. But she stopped herself and instead pivoted to the cashier, who smiled as she walked up.

"Good day to you," the woman said. Her dark eyes crinkled in the corners. "How can I help you?"

Gemma had to swallow before she could talk. "I'd like to see Cináed, please."

The cashier's dark eyebrows rose slightly. "Just one moment. I'll get him."

As she walked through a door behind her, Gemma took a step back. It felt as if every eye in the store was on her, although she knew that wasn't true. Since she wasn't purchasing anything, she moved away from the area.

Her fingers fiddled with the handle of her purse, toying with a frayed string from the stitching. The longer she stood by herself, the more nervous she became. It was partly due to the fact she was out in public. After so many years of keeping to herself, it was difficult to be around others.

But the true reason was because she feared that Cináed had gotten her hopes up. There was a very real chance that he knew nothing more than what he'd already told her. It could all be a ploy to try and get...

What? What did he want? Her mind went blank. She didn't have an answer, but there were enough others who had tried to exploit her that it became a habit to keep everyone at a distance.

Essentially, she was a hermit. And that was a hard habit to break.

"Gemma."

She turned at the sound of her name to find Cináed. There was surprise in his gaze at the sight of her. And if she wasn't mistaken, there was also happiness there. As if her arrival had given him pleasure.

"I'm glad you came," he said.

She kept her focus on his face. Mainly because it was difficult to look at anything else. Why did he have to be so handsome?

Cináed grinned at her silence. "Come. We can talk in private."

Yes. Private. That's what she wanted. No one else needed to hear their exchange.

She fell in step behind him. Trepidation swallowed her as she walked around the counter and through the doorway the cashier had disappeared through to get Cináed. There was something about being at Dreagan that felt as if she had walked into another world.

And passing through the doorway gave her the impression that she was entering an area not seen by anyone other than those at Dreagan. Almost like a secret section.

It was silly. Her overactive imagination could create all sorts of things. Just like that figure in the storm when she was little. It didn't help that she had seen the video about the supposed dragons at Dreagan.

Maybe she should have been a writer with her imagination. It would have given her the same kind of reclusiveness that she'd come to depend on. But honestly, she couldn't see herself doing anything but being a researcher. Her topics changed often, allowing her to delve into things she wouldn't have otherwise known about.

Cináed looked over his shoulder at her. Almost as if making sure that she was still there. What did he think? That she would disappear?

She had to admit, she was thinking about it. Gemma didn't know where he was taking her—or to who. She liked to be prepared in any situation. Every time she had come in contact with Cináed, it had been anything but.

And she wasn't sure how to handle that.

It disrupted her tidy world. It made chaos out of order.

It kept her constantly on guard, wondering what he might say and how she might handle it. So far, she hadn't done very well at all.

In no time they walked out of the building. The dark clouds from the storm remained, reluctant to leave and hinting at more rain. She tried not to let that bother her. Surely she would be able to keep the fears from her childhood at bay around others.

Surely.

Hopefully.

Please God.

Cináed walked down a path that was hidden from the parking lot. She looked around her, making sure she could get back if she needed to leave in a hurry. There was nothing like taking a wrong turn in a new place when she wanted to make an exit.

"You're safe," he said as he slowed, allowing her to come even with him.

Gemma shot him a hard look. "By whose standards?"

A small smile played about his lips. "I'll earn your trust, Gemma. I promise."

She tried not to let his words affect her, but they did. Greatly. No one had said such a thing to her. Ever. At every turn Cináed surprised her, keeping her off guard. Maybe that's exactly what he wanted.

Her thoughts stopped when they went through a row of tall hedges and she saw the manor. It was...enormous. The dark gray stone stood against the bright green foliage and craggy mountains, imposing and formidable. And somehow...welcoming.

She couldn't explain it. It was the most peculiar feeling. There wasn't an ounce of fear within her when Cináed opened the door and she walked through it.

Inside, she was taken aback by the richness of color. The wealth was obvious in subtle ways—the rugs, artwork (all with dragons, she noticed), and the furniture. It was a place she wanted to explore, learning the hidden parts of the house and discovering its secrets.

Because she knew it had many.

Her head turned to Cináed. He also had secrets. She saw that clearly now. How had she missed it before?

"Welcome to Dreagan."

Chapter Seven

She was there. Actually at Dreagan.

Cináed didn't know what it was that had convinced Gemma to come, but he was excited that she had. Yet he knew he had his work cut out for him.

She was aloof and untrusting. Not that he blamed her. One night had altered the course of her entire life, causing her to be withdrawn and detached from society. He understood her more than she could imagine, though it wasn't as if he could tell her that he hid something as well.

If she had gotten so upset at seeing her mother's locket, he could only imagine what Gemma would do if he told her he was actually a dragon.

"How did you know who I was?" she demanded.

Straight to the point. Cináed shot her a quick grin as he motioned her to continue with him. He decided it was best to take her to the library where Ryder and Merrill had put everything while he had gone to get Gemma.

"I was doing a bit of research for Dreagan," he began.

She interrupted to ask, "What kind of research?"

"We're looking for...a group, but suffice it to say that in order to find the origins, I've been looking through old newspapers." He stopped and opened the library door for her. Once she moved over the threshold, he followed. "I found the article about you and your family."

Gemma stopped, her perusal of the library halted as she turned to look at him. She quirked a brow. "And?"

Cináed realized that the only way he would reach her was with honesty. "The article was intriguing, but it was your picture that grabbed me. There was something in your eyes that refused to let me go."

"Fear."

He shook his head. "That was there, aye, but it was something more. You suffered something terrible, something that you have kept to yourself all these years."

"And you want me to tell you. Is that it?" she demanded, bowing up for an argument.

"I would like to know what happened, because I think you have insight that could help unlock things so you can have answers, but I'm no' going to ask you to tell me anything you doona want to. The look the photographer captured has haunted me. It propelled me to dig deep into what happened. Your story went along with that until it suddenly didna."

She held his gaze, refusing to reply.

Cináed wanted to move the lock of ginger hair out of her eyelashes, but he didn't dare go any closer to her. She was like a frightened animal. Any moment now she would bolt. He could sense it. So he kept his distance.

At first he thought she hadn't changed because she hadn't been trying to impress him, but when she turned in the shop and he saw the remnants of tear tracks, he knew it was the need for answers that spurred her to him and nothing more. Though he had to admit he was a little disappointed.

"You changed your name," he continued. "Smart move. You also covered your tracks well."

"Obviously not well enough if you found me."

He twisted his lips. "To be fair, I dug deeper than most."

"I might be impressed, but I wanted to stay hidden."

"Nothing goes past us. Your secrets remain with me."

She lifted her gaze and looked around slowly. "As well as everyone at Dreagan." Gemma's gaze then returned to him, daring him to deny it.

He bowed his head to her. "We are a close family. Whatever secrets find their way here never leave."

"How rare," she murmured.

Cináed knew she didn't believe him. That was fine. He would prove it to her. He walked to the table and the newspaper with the article and picture of her. He looked into the eyes of the photo—the same eyes that stared back at him each time he met Gemma's gaze.

"You ran into me because I was trying to get a look at you," he confessed. "I had no intention of talking to you then. As I said, I expected you to turn the other way."

She came to stand on the opposite side of the table. Her fingers lightly rested on the wood as she took in all the articles and other documents lying about. "Your research was thorough."

"Despite everything I read, I knew I needed to go to the isle."

A shiver went through her that she couldn't hide. "I've not seen it since the day they took me away."

"The buildings still stand, though barely. The house was searched, but nothing has been touched except what the elements have ravaged."

Her blue eyes lifted to his. "You found the locket."

"We dove, searching for anything."

"I've had others do that three different times. Even the authorities conducted searches. How did you find it?"

He shrugged, unable to tell her. "Luck, I suppose."

She shook her head. "I don't believe that."

"I'm glad I was able to find something. I'm sorry it upset you."

Her eyes darted away for a moment. "It's all I have left of my family. I should have thanked you instead of reacting the way I did."

Cináed shifted the papers to show the map of the small isle. "The locket was found here," he said as he pointed to the waters about a quarter mile from land.

She stared at the map for so long in silence that he wondered if she was lost in memories.

"I can take you there, if you'd like," he offered.

Gemma jerked back as if slapped. "No."

Her reply had come out in a near shout. If he'd had any doubt that something horrible had happened that night, it was gone now.

"I want to find the answers for you," he offered. "Do I have your permission to keep looking?"

She turned away, walking to a shelf of books. Her arms were wrapped around her. Strength radiated from her, but at the same time she looked vulnerable.

"You doona have to do this alone," he said.

She gave a bark of laughter, but still didn't look at him. "Do you know how many reporters and police said those same words to me? No one wants to do this for me. They want to do it for themselves." She twisted around, locking her gaze with his. "Even you."

"I admit I want to solve the mystery. The more I look into that night, the more questions I have. You're the only one who holds the answers. Whether you believe it or no', I have a driving need to see this through. I can no' explain why I have to know what happened, but I do know that it's important."

"And you always listen to your feelings?"

"Always. Surely you do the same."

She blew out a breath and turned to face him. All the ire had gone out of her. She looked tired and crushed under the emotions she'd been through that morning. "I do."

"I understand your hesitancy. I would be the same. Keep your story. All I ask is that you be with me as I keep looking. Help lead me in the right direction."

Her gaze searched his. "What do you get out of this?"

"Nothing other than the satisfaction that you can finally rest easy and stop looking over your shoulder in fear. Once you have the answers, you willna be worried about what others find."

She bit her lip, considering his words.

"Also," he added, "I can make sure that no one ever finds out that you changed your name."

"Blackmail?" she asked, though there was no heat in her words.

He shook his head. "I'll have it done right now, regardless if you help me or not."

"Prove it," she said and crossed her arms over her chest.

One side of Cináed's lips lifted in a grin. "Come with me."

He turned on his heel and walked from the library to the stairs. They ascended the steps until they reached the floor with Ryder's computer room. Gemma kept up with him, her gaze moving about, but she never stopped or asked any questions.

"*Ryder,*" Cináed said through the mental link dragons had. "*I'm bringing Gemma up to you.*"

"*Thanks for the warning,*" Ryder replied.

Once they reached the door to Ryder's office, Cináed knocked and opened it. He swept his arm forward, telling Gemma to walk ahead of him.

"Welcome," Ryder said when they came around the screens.

"Uh...hello," Gemma replied as her gaze swept over the numerous monitors.

Cináed slid his eyes from Gemma to Ryder. "Could you please make sure that no one can discover what Gemma changed her last name to?"

"Consider it done," Ryder said as he began moving his fingers over the keyboard.

The screens flashed and were filled with all of the files on Gemma. It took just a few keystrokes before the pages vanished.

Ryder then turned his chair to them and smiled. "There you go. No one will ever find you."

A small frown formed on Gemma's forehead as she looked from the screens to Ryder then to Cináed. "Thank you both."

"I told you that you were safe here," Cináed said.

She took a deep breath, her gaze dropping to the floor. "I'm not safe anywhere."

Cináed exchanged a look with Ryder. Neither said anything about Gemma's comment. Cináed gave a nod to Ryder and trailed behind Gemma when she walked to the door.

Once in the hallway, she stopped and faced him. "No one does things like this for nothing."

"Some do."

"Not the people I've run across. Why are you helping me?"

"I told you. It's something I have to see through. For you and for me."

She frowned, her head cocking to the side. "Who are you?"

"A friend. If you'll have me."

Gemma stared at him a long moment before she looked away, shaking her head. "I don't have friends."

"That can change, you know. Anytime."

Her gaze returned to him. "I've not exactly been friendly to you."

"You have no reason to trust me. Your reaction to things is natural."

"I don't do well around people."

Cináed grinned. "I doona either, actually."

She snorted loudly. "I don't believe that for a minute."

"Trust me. It's verra true."

Gemma walked aimlessly down the corridor. She stopped after a few steps and slowly turned to him. "What would you want me to do?"

"Whatever you're comfortable with."

"I'm not comfortable with any of it. I never have been."

He nodded and walked a few steps closer to her. "You're afraid. You doona have to be anymore."

"I'm terrified. And it will never go away."

"If you find the answers, it just might. A child's brain sees things different than adults. Things you didna understand back then may focus in a completely different light."

She pressed her lips together. "I hope you're right."

"Does that mean you'll help?"

"What do I have to lose?"

He fought not to smile because he was so happy. "Nothing. But you have everything to gain."

She frowned again. "It's not just coincidence that I chose the village to live, is it? It feels...."

"Like this meeting was meant to happen?" he offered.

"Yes."

He'd felt like that since the moment he found her picture. "I think it's because it was meant to happen. I think together we will solve the mystery of what happened to your family that night."

"I'd come to accept that I'd never know." A ghost of a smile tugged at her lips. "I'm almost afraid to hope that everything will get cleared up, because I've been disappointed so many times."

Cináed smiled at her. "No matter how long it takes, we'll get the answers."

Chapter Eight

Could it finally happen? Gemma almost didn't allow herself to hope. But there was something in Cináed's gray eyes that gave her the courage to take a chance.

"All right," she said and licked her lips, unsure of what to do or say now. Something sweeping and potent had occurred with just a few words between them and she wasn't sure how to digest it all. "I guess I better get home."

Gemma turned and began walking toward the stairs. She really hoped she could maneuver her way through the maze of the manor to find the door. She was certain she could get to her car from there. It was just getting outside that was the tricky part.

"You doona want to start now?"

Cináed's words stopped her in her tracks. She took a deep breath. What a dolt she was. Of course he'd want to start now. Why hadn't she thought of that?

Because you haven't figured out which way is up when you're with him.

He came to stand in front of her. "If you want to leave, I'll walk you out. However, if you wish to begin today, we can. It's up to you."

There had been very little in her life that had been in her control—and this wasn't one of them. Cináed drove this train. He had from the moment she backed into him. Usually that annoyed her, but not this time for some reason.

"Of course."

Cináed raised a brow. "You doona sound sure. Would you rather come back later?"

"I don't know what I want to do," she confessed.

Gemma covered her face with her hands and took in a breath

before she lowered her arms and met Cináed's troubled eyes.

"Perhaps starting today isna a good idea," he said.

She shook her head. "No, no. It's fine."

"Take as long as you need," he continued. "When you're ready, you can let me know."

Gemma issued another shake of her head. "I appreciate your words. I'm sure I'm coming off as... Well, I don't even know what you might think of me, but it isn't good. Seeing the locket was...difficult."

"I'm sure it was."

"That, coupled with your offer, along with the fact that I usually do everything on my own, and I'm struggling to find my footing."

Cináed nodded slowly, looking abashed. "I apologize. I shouldna have pushed you. It's just a puzzle I feel compelled to figure out."

"Not at all," she hurried to say. "You're trying to help, and I've not been appreciative of that."

"I can no' listen to any more," a man said as he came up the stairs. His dark blue eyes met Cináed's before they swung to her. His dirty blond hair was cut in the latest style, and he raked his hand through the long length on top. "You've both apologized. Now someone make a decision."

Cináed sighed loudly. "Gemma, this is Merrill. Merrill, Gemma."

She nodded in Merrill's direction by way of a hello.

"He's the one who found the locket," Cináed explained.

Gemma's gaze jerked back to Merrill. "Did you find anything else?"

Merrill's eyes briefly lowered to the ground. "Afraid no'. I was lucky to discover the necklace. I just happened to move debris that allowed a bit of the metal to shine through."

"You both gave me back a piece of my family. I can never repay that," she told them. "Thank you doesn't seem to be enough."

Cináed smiled. "It's more than enough."

"We want to help," Merrill said. "Let us."

With both of them—tall and gorgeous—staring at her, there was only one thing she could say. "I'd like that."

Merrill slapped his hands together and rubbed. "Now that that's settled, how about we discuss returning to the isle?"

That was one place Gemma knew she would never return to. Her mind was stuck on that thought, so she wasn't able to get any words out. Thankfully, Cináed didn't have that problem.

"No' yet," he said. "Besides, Gemma is deciding if she'd like to return and do this another day."

Her eyes lifted, meeting the clear gray ones of Cináed. Another day? Right. Like that was going to happen. She wouldn't be able to concentrate on anything else now that she had seen the extent of what Cináed had gone to for.... Well, he said it was because her picture stirred him and he wanted answers.

But *why*?

"You don't know me," she told him. "You have no reason to help or even be concerned about my family. The people I've paid to look for things have given me less. I don't think I believe it's just something you feel you have to do."

Merrill ran a hand down his face as he turned on his heel. "I'll be in the library," he said before he walked away.

Cináed didn't reply until Merrill was gone, and the entire time, he kept his gaze on her. It made Gemma shift uncomfortably, but she wasn't sure why. There was no anger, condemnation, or derision in his eyes. Maybe it was the way it felt as if he were studying her. Almost as if he were determining how much he could trust her.

Finally, he said, "You doona know me either. I've thrown a tremendous amount your way, and you've taken it all graciously."

Gemma wasn't so sure of that, but she didn't interrupt him to dispute it.

"I've given you no reason to trust me, so how could I expect you to freely accept my explanation?" He shot her a crooked smile.

He turned and began walking. She quickly fell in step with him. It was her curiosity about what he might show her next that had her following. And oddly enough, she wasn't shunning his presence as she normally did with anyone she had to spend more than a few moments with.

She found herself staring at him as they made their way down the stairs, wondering what made him different. It could be the money. But she'd interacted with others who were just as rich. While his handsomeness exceeded anyone's she'd ever met, it wasn't that either.

He glanced at her, his brows drawing together when he caught her looking at him. "Something wrong?"

"I'm trying to figure you out," she admitted.

He laughed softly and took her through the house to a kitchen that was larger than her entire cottage. He motioned to the table, and she stopped and pulled a heavy chair out to sit.

"Tea?" he asked.

She nodded, unable to look away from him. He looked comfortable in the kitchen. Obviously this wasn't the first time he had made tea for someone. And for some strange reason, that pleased her.

"I was going to take you outside but the weather isna cooperating."

Gemma was surrounded by windows throughout the house, but she hadn't looked through one of them. When she moved her gaze to the large window over the sink, she saw the sheets of rain coming down at an angle from the wind.

All that was missing was the thunder and lightning and she would be transported back to the night her family was lost.

"You doona like storms."

She jerked at how close Cináed was. She had been so lost in thought she hadn't heard or seen him. Then she saw the cup of tea in front of her and she realized she had been lost in thought for some time. She spotted the milk and sugar bowl and reached for the milk, pouring a hefty amount in her cup as Cináed sat next to her.

The silence felt like a wet blanket sucking all the air from her. She stirred her tea and gently set the spoon aside. Then she raised the cup to her lips and took a sip. The tea was exceptionally good, but then she was at Dreagan so she expected that.

"Rain doesn't bother me," she admitted. Her eyes lifted to his face. "It's the raging storms that I'd rather not be around."

He gave a nod. "It reminds you of that night."

"Yes. I end up reliving it all over each time a storm comes."

Cináed's brows drew together. "There was such a storm last eve."

She didn't say anything. There was no need for a response. The truth sat between them. Gemma lowered her gaze to the cup, becoming engrossed in the simple white design. No floral pattern for those at Dreagan. That struck her as humorous.

While waiting, hoping that Cináed would say something, she drank her tea. A few seconds later, he let out a whistle. That had her lifting her eyes to him to find him grinning.

"Wait," he said when she parted her lips to ask what that was.

She heard a commotion that sounded like something large was coming down the stairs. She tried to determine what the scratching sound was, then she saw the massive Great Dane running on the wood floor. A smile split over her face as the dog stopped and let Cináed pet him before he turned to Gemma.

The moment her hands sank into the soft fur of the dog, all her worries disappeared. She was soon laughing while trying to evade the Great Dane, who was doing his best to lick her.

"Duke has the run of the place," Cináed said. "He's Callie and Hal's, but he has his favorites. While he seems to have taken a liking to V, I give him food. So he likes me a lot."

"That's why he comes so quickly when you whistle," she said.

Cináed nodded as he laughed and patted the dog. "Exactly. I know how to win over animals."

And people apparently, too. But she didn't say the words. Perhaps she should have. Cináed went out of his way to make her feel comfortable. If she wasn't so distrusting of people she might find it sweet, but she kept looking for whatever angle he was using to get to her. And she hated that she was like that.

Gemma refused to think of that more, though. She focused on the dog and the joy having him with her brought. Duke sat beside her, panting, while she continually petted him. Ever since Daisy and that night, the only way she had gotten through each day was with a dog beside her.

She and Cináed shared a smile. He made it easy to relax with him, and while he wanted to know her story, he didn't push. Not once did he ask about that night or what information she could give him to help in his search.

All he had asked was that she be with them to give what little she felt she could. Since she didn't want to talk about any of it, they weren't likely to learn much of anything. Unless she told them all of it.

Except she wasn't sure she could.

Her smile faded and she found herself wrapping her arms around Duke. She rested her head against his. "Dogs are so accepting. They don't ask questions. They love unconditionally and only want to be loved in return."

"I know there must have been others who only befriended you to see if they could extract information," Cináed said. "I can also see why you are so guarded. It's warranted. You must go with your instincts. You'll know when the time is right."

She straightened to look at him. "It's been easy to put the past out of my mind, to try and forget it."

"The past never loosens its hold."

Her head cocked to the side at his words. Then she whispered,

"You know what it feels like?"

"To want to forget but be unable to do so?" He gave a nod as his face filled with sadness. "Verra much so."

"You keep your secret close, don't you?"

He gave her a melancholy smile. "Always."

She knew without asking that the secret was a heavy one to bear. Maybe even weightier than her own. Just as she was about to ask what it was, she realized that she couldn't. Not only because she herself refused to share, but because secrets that substantial had to be freely told by the one who carried them.

Gemma reached over and put her hand on Cináed's arm. Whatever bond that was between them strengthened with the knowledge that each held such a hefty burden.

Chapter Nine

The moment between Cináed and Gemma was broken when Duke bounded away. It wasn't long before Cináed heard the voices of some of the mates making their way into the manor. One look at Gemma and he could see she was ready to bolt.

"We have a large family at Dreagan. Some are married. The commotion you hear is a few of the women returning. I can introduce you if you'd like, or we can make our escape."

"Escape, please," she murmured.

He held out his hand, and to his surprise, she took it without hesitation. Cináed then quickly maneuvered them out of the kitchen and behind a large pillar as Darcy, Rachel, and Grace turned the corner.

Cináed looked down at Gemma to find her staring at the women oddly. Almost like she was trying to figure out how they could interact so easily with each other.

As interesting as that was, he was very aware that their hands were still joined. He wasn't sure she was conscious of it so he didn't plan on saying anything. Besides, he liked the feel of her palm against his.

When the women had disappeared in the kitchen, Gemma turned her head to him. "Thank you."

"No problem," he replied.

She looked down, and to his disappointment, pulled her hand from his. "Can you take me back to the library?"

"Of course."

They made their way there. Cináed rolled his eyes when he saw Merrill asleep on one of the couches. Gemma ignored him and went at once to the table to look through everything again. Cináed stood to the side watching her.

She moved things into stacks. When she finished, she shoved a rather large stack toward him, and without looking up said, "There is not a single truth in these."

He took the papers and tossed them on the floor. If anyone knew what was lies and what wasn't, it was the only one alive who had been witness to it—Gemma herself.

"These are people that I hired for myself. They then turned around and sold their story," she explained about the next stack.

Thankfully it was a small one, but there was no mistaking the hard tone in her voice. She had been betrayed more times than he knew. It was becoming more and more clear why the walls around her were so thick. And he was ready to help her strengthen them himself, because no one should go through the things that she had.

Especially alone.

"Did they find anything useful?" he asked.

She gave a little shrug. "Nothing more than I already knew myself."

Cináed looked over the names. He grabbed the laptop that he'd brought down and opened it. A few minutes later his search of the first name brought up the man's website and all his accolades for work as a private investigator. A look at the rates had Cináed seeing red.

"He charges a fortune."

Gemma glanced at the computer and issued another shrug. "I thought he was worth it."

Cináed saved the website to do more of a deeper search later. The next few minutes he spent looking at the other three people and discovered all were top in their fields and charged exorbitant prices.

And each of them had betrayed Gemma.

He straightened and looked at her. "Please tell me you had them sign non-disclosure agreements."

"Of course. I hired a very pricy solicitor to handle that, and yet when I tried to sue them, they managed to turn it against me."

"Have the suits been settled?"

She gave a shake of her head. "I'm about ready to give up."

"No," Cináed stated. "Doona give them the satisfaction. I can help with that."

Confusion filled Gemma's face. "Why?"

"Because I've never liked when someone takes advantage of others. I can do something, and if you'll allow me, I will see to it. Fire your solicitor."

She put a hand on her hip and regarded him with a look filled with puzzlement. "Are you a solicitor?"

"Actually, I am."

Her eyes widened. "You have a practice?"

"As you can imagine, there is much to handle for Dreagan. Vaughan is master of all things legal, but I was curious about the field, so I got my degree so I could help him."

She nodded slowly. "And you make it sound like you went down and bought a car."

"I didna mean to," he said with a chuckle. "Things just come easy to me."

"Like?" she pressed.

He lifted one shoulder. "Anything. I could give you a list of the many different jobs around Dreagan that others are in charge of. I'm the one who goes to each to learn how it's done and masters it to nearly the level of the others."

"Then you move on to something else?" she asked in disbelief.

Cináed inwardly winced. Perhaps he should have thought about rewording that. "Aye."

"And you retain everything?"

"I do."

"That's...impressive. I admit, I'm a bit jealous of your skill."

Relief swept through him, allowing a wide smile to pull at his lips. "I have a lot of skills. Make use of them."

"You really want to help with the lawsuits?"

"Absolutely," he stated. "Something doesna add up with your solicitor, the NDA, and these people who seemingly got away with writing these articles for, I'm guessing, quite a sum of money."

Her lips twisted. "It's not about the money. It's about them giving me their word, signing a legal—binding—document, and then going behind my back."

Cináed made a mental note to dig deeper into Gemma's solicitor and the connection with those who wrote the pieces.

"I should pay you something," she said.

He frowned at her. "I think you've lost out on enough money. Besides, I doona need it."

"It's the principle of it though. You have no reason to give me such help for free."

"My reason is that I want to."

Her lips flattened as she studied him. "I'm going to agree but only if you promise that if things become more than you expect that you'll come to me and we'll work out an arrangement for payment."

"I accept." Cináed gladly agreed because he knew that was never going to happen.

They shook on it then, but already he was planning on the action he was going to take. No one had stood up for—or with—Gemma all these years. Someone needed to do it, and he wanted to be that person.

He wanted her to look at him with a welcoming smile instead of a guarded one. He wanted her to greet him without wariness, without wondering what he was after.

In short, he wanted her to trust him.

"My mother took off the locket to entice me to get on the boat," Gemma suddenly said.

Cináed's mind came to a halt as he waited to see if she would continue. Thankfully, she did.

"I didn't want to go. The isle was all I'd ever known. I was happy there. It was home. My home. I didn't understand why we had to leave or why I couldn't take all of my things." She turned her head away to look at the empty fireplace. "I wanted to bring all of my toys, but I was only allowed to bring three items. So, I did what most children would do, I made a fuss. Da was yelling for Mum to get downstairs. She knew how much I loved the locket, so she said if I came with her that the locket would be mine, and I'd get new toys. She never took the locket off. Ever. And she was going to give it to me."

Gemma's gaze slid back to him. "We went downstairs and we were at the boat when I heard my dog bark. I wasn't going anywhere without Daisy. Da and Kyle were already on the boat, and Mum was tugging me, trying to force me on. I slipped out of her hold. She took off the locket and held it out to me. I wanted it so badly, and I knew it wouldn't take me long to get Daisy. I thought I could get my dog *and* have the necklace."

"You went back for the dog," Cináed said as things began to fall into place. "That's why you were no' on the boat."

She shook her head sadly. "That was the last time I saw my family."

"It's also why you have such a fondness for canines. Daisy was all you had until you were found."

"When she died, it nearly destroyed me."

"I've been in that position before."

Her pale blue eyes held such despair and heartache that he wanted to pull her against him and hold her, but he didn't dare. He had made great headway with her. To touch her now might irreparably damage that.

The sound of laughter nearby made Gemma jump, reminding Cináed that she was used to being by herself. Perhaps bringing her here hadn't been a good idea.

"We can pack all this up and take it to your place if you'd rather," he offered.

She bit her lip. "You would be all right with that?"

"I'm here to help you, Gemma. We can do this anywhere."

"Then, yes, please. I would very much like to return home."

He gave her a nod. "It'll take me just a moment to pack all of this up. Do you want to wait for me or go on ahead?"

She hesitated. "I don't have much in the way of food. I should probably stop at the store."

"Doona concern yourself on my account. Everything will be fine."

"I don't believe most people when they say that, but for some reason, I do with you."

"Because it will be."

She smiled easily. "I'll meet you at my house then."

"That you will."

Cináed walked her to her car and watched her drive off. When he returned to the library Merrill had already gathered everything and put it in a messenger bag along with one of Ryder's laptops.

"Thanks," Cináed said.

Merrill stepped in front of him. "You know I heard the exchange between you and Gemma."

"I assumed."

"She asked you, but now I am. Why are you wanting to help this mortal?"

Cináed shrugged and shifted the bag from one hand to the other. "As I said, it's a feeling, a drive I can no' ignore. Something led me to Gemma."

"You think that there is some connection between what happened to her family and us?"

"I doona know. It's what I'm hoping to determine, but even you have to admit that people doona disappear as her family did."

Merrill's lips twisted. "A lot can happen in the water. Between the currents and animals, there would be nothing left for anyone to find."

"All these years, aye, I agree with you. Three weeks after? I doona believe that. Even if the storm slammed the boat against rocks anywhere near the isle, something would've been found. And I keep coming back to the fact that the parents wouldna leave their daughter. Now we know for certain they didna."

"You're taking her word for it?"

"I am."

Merrill crossed his arms over his chest. "She was a child. How can you trust what she remembers?"

"The same gut feeling that led me to her. Just as I know that she's no' told us everything. There is more. Whether it's what happened that night or over the three weeks before she was found, there are missing parts of the story."

"Since I didna believe she would share what she did, if anyone can get it out of her, it's you," Merrill said.

Cináed wasn't so sure. "I doona think it'll be as easy as you say."

"When you return to the isle, because we both know you will, doona go without me."

"I willna."

As Cináed walked away, Merrill said, "And doona think I didna see you looking at her as if you want to eat her up."

Cináed flipped him off and kept walking.

Chapter Ten

Gemma drove as fast as she dared on the slick streets back to her cottage. In her rush to get out of the car, she forgot to unbuckle her seatbelt, which kept her from actually exiting. Then, when she tried to unbuckle it, she somehow managed to become entangled with it, causing her to fall out of her car onto her hands.

She jumped up, thankful that no one was there to see it. But if she thought the seatbelt was finished with her, she was wrong. It twisted around her foot. This time she managed to stay upright, hopping around like an idiot until she was finally—mercifully—free.

Gemma slammed the door, glaring at the offensive piece and thinking of the wasted seconds she could've been inside picking up. She happened to glance down at her attire. No. She could've been changing.

She stormed off toward the front door, not sure if she was still angry at her car or the fact that she wanted to change. It had been way too long since she had given consideration to what anyone—especially a man—thought about the clothes she wore. And yet that's exactly what she was doing.

Then again, Cináed wasn't just any man. He was helping her find answers, and to top it off he was going to take her case against the individuals who had disregarded the NDAs. She still couldn't believe it.

And a part of her truly believed that Cináed had some kind of agenda. Though she wasn't so sure it was about her. She had been around enough people who sought something from her that she was able to discern it pretty quickly. Cináed was different. He did want something, but she wasn't sure exactly what that was yet.

She had yet to decipher how helping her fit into his plans, but she would. Patience was a virtue that she had mastered. For once, she felt as if she was the one who was actually getting the benefit with a partnership. It was a new experience, and quite frankly she wasn't sure how to handle it.

Gemma tossed her keys into the glass bowl on the table by the front door. She plopped her purse next to it and took a step before she lifted her foot and tugged off her boots. She ran into her bedroom, placed the boots in her closet and hurriedly yanked off her clothes.

Her fingers ran across the clothes hanging in her closet. She didn't have much. It was easier to pack light when one moved so frequently. And wouldn't you know that there wasn't a single shirt she wanted to wear.

Then she remembered the black one that she always felt good in. She searched the closet but it wasn't there. A sigh left her when she remembered it was in a pile to be washed.

"Of course it is."

She settled for a dark gray pullover that didn't cling too tightly to her but still showed off her curves. Not that she wanted Cináed to notice her.

Liar.

Ignoring her subconscious, she found a pair of jeans and slipped them on. Then she rushed into the bathroom and began to brush out her hair. She'd gotten halfway through when there was a knock.

Gemma quickly finished and walked from the bathroom. She happened to look down and saw that for some reason she only had on one sock. She removed it and shoved it into her purse as she reached the door.

There she paused to take a deep breath before opening it. Her gaze landed on Cináed, who gave her an incredibly sexy crooked grin that caused her stomach to flutter. She put a hand on her abdomen to stop it before she stepped aside to allow him to enter.

His gaze moved over her, though he didn't say anything about her change of clothes. She wasn't sure if she was happy about that or not. Gemma decided to let it go and focus on other things.

Cináed walked to the table and set the messenger bag in the chair. It took her a moment to realize what he looked at. It wasn't until she went to the table that she caught sight of the locket. It didn't look as if it had spent the last twenty-two years in the sea hidden from sight.

"I cleaned it," he said into the silence.

Gemma lifted her gaze to him. "Thank you."

She had yet to touch it. Frankly, a part of her was afraid to. If seeing it had sent her spiraling back to that night what would putting it on do? She wasn't ready to discover that.

Gemma cleared her throat and rubbed her hands on her hips, letting her palms scrape against the denim. "I...uh...I don't know where to begin."

"You already have," Cináed replied. "Tell me about the rest of the piles you made from the papers at Dreagan."

Yes! Something she could focus on. "I have looked at each of those articles more times than I can remember. The couple who took me in tried to hide them from me, but I was able to get the articles other ways. I hid them from everyone. Sometimes I read them, sometimes I would just put them together for a day that I knew I would need them. It became a habit. For as long as I can remember, I researched everything about myself and my family. I suppose that's how I fell into my career."

"Can you tell me how you chose Clacher when you changed your surname?"

His question took her by surprise. That was something no one had ever asked her about, but she could tell that it meant something to Cináed. Perhaps this was part of the angle he was after.

Gemma shrugged. "It was no great endeavor. I saw it in some papers I found at the house on the isle when I was there by myself. It stayed with me, I suppose. When I made the name change, it was the first name that popped into my head. And it seemed to fit. So I used it."

"I see," Cináed said, nodding absently as he glanced at the table.

"Were you expecting another answer?"

He drew in a quick breath and twisted his lips. "I wouldna say that."

"But the Clacher name means something to you."

Cináed didn't deny it. He stared at her a moment before he said, "Aye. It does."

"You think my family has something to do with them? Is that why I found that name?"

He scratched the side of his head and wrinkled his nose. "No' as far as I can see. We did a genealogy search of your family. You are no' connected to the Clachers in any way."

Gemma found her lips parting ready to deny that when some voice inside her head screamed at her to remain silent.

"What?" Cináed pressed as he peered at her. "What just went through your mind? What were you about to say?"

She shrugged and looked anywhere but his gray eyes. "I'm not really sure."

He pulled out a chair and sat while resting his forearms on the table. "I know there is still much I need to do in order to gain your trust. I'm prepared to do that, but if you are no' willing to trust me, then this may no' work."

Gemma turned away. Her gaze landed on the cup of tea she'd made before Cináed had arrived earlier. She walked to get it and rinsed it out at the sink. He didn't say a word as she completed the task.

She put her hands on the counter and closed her eyes for a heartbeat. "You have every right to say that." She then turned to face him. "You want me to share, but it's only fair that you do the same."

"I'm sorry?" he asked, a frown marring his forehead.

"What's your interest in the Clacher name? It's obvious it holds some importance to you."

Cináed pressed his lips together and nodded before a smile curved his lips. "You're right, of course. Like you, I'm used to keeping things about myself secret."

"Because people want to exploit your name and money? Or is it the connection to one of the most well-known brands around the world?"

"Something like that," he replied.

It was one of those answers that Gemma knew well. The kind that gave a reply but didn't really respond to anything. She held his gaze and lifted a brow. To her surprise, Cináed chuckled.

"It seems we both need to learn to trust," he said. "I'll tell you what I can, because there are some things I can no' share."

It was the first time anyone had ever told her they couldn't tell her something, and she didn't like it. At all. Was this how others viewed her? She was getting a dose of her own medicine, and it left a very bad taste in her mouth.

"Sounds fair," she replied.

Cináed smiled and motioned to the table. Gemma pushed away from the counter and took the chair opposite him at the round table. Even sitting she was aware of how wide his shoulders were and how tall he was. He dwarfed her already small cottage, but at the same time, she found that she liked him there. He seemed at home in her place as much as he did in the opulence and grandeur of Dreagan Manor.

And she suspected there were few men who could pull that off. It was just another way that Cináed was different.

Gemma waited for him to begin. The frown he wore intensified as the seconds ticked by. "Would you rather not tell me?" she finally asked.

He met her gaze and said, "That's no' it at all. I'm trying to figure out where to begin the story."

"The beginning is usually the best."

He gave her a look of regret.

"Ah. I see." She nodded. "Give me the facts that you can. We'll make it work."

That seemed to ease his mind. He sat back in the chair then, relaxing. "The Clachers that I'm interested in come from the Isle of Eigg."

Since Eigg was in the same cluster of islands of the Hebrides that included the isle she'd grown up on, she realized why he had made the connection. "A family connection?"

"No' to mine, but to the woman married to one of my brothers."

Gemma crossed one leg over the other. "I see. Are you tracing a family history?"

"Aye. The Clachers were a verra prominent family in the past, but there was an event that wiped them all out."

Her brows shot up. "An event?"

Cináed blew out a breath. "The fact is, someone murdered every one of them."

Gemma's mouth fell open in shock at the news. "Do you know why?"

"It was in retaliation. The Clachers were no' just respected, but also feared by some because they had become so powerful."

"If all of them were wiped out, then anyone using that name would instantly call your attention," she surmised.

Cináed smiled. "Exactly. Couple that with your story, and I couldna walk away without looking deeper into things."

"Well, I hate to disappoint, but there is nothing to the name I chose. Like I said, I found it on some papers and it stuck."

"What kind of papers?" he pressed.

She shrugged, searching her mind. "I don't remember. Honestly, as a kid, I probably wouldn't have even realized what they were."

"Do you remember where these papers were?"

"In the attic. There were boxes hidden in a dresser. I searched every nook and cranny of that house, so anything that looked hidden like that I immediately went through. It wasn't as if I had anyone telling me to stay out of it."

Cináed leaned forward, his arms folding on the table. "Can you recall if there were a lot of boxes?"

"Just a couple. Three at the most, if I remember right." She realized where his questioning was headed. "You want to go back to the isle, don't you?"

He bowed his head to her. "It would be good to go through and find those papers."

With everything he was doing for her, who was she to deny him such a thing? "Go find what you need."

"You willna come with me?"

She glanced at the locket. "No."

Chapter Eleven

It's what Cináed had expected. Still, he'd thought Gemma might change her mind and be willing to return to the isle. Obviously, he'd been wrong.

"I can tell you exactly where to look," she told him.

He issued a quick smile to let her know that her concession was fine. "I'd appreciate that."

"You're disappointed."

"I'm no' going to push you to do something that you are no' comfortable with."

She crossed her arms over her chest and cocked her head at him. "But you think I should go."

"I wasna there that night. You were. You know what you can and can no' handle."

"I've had others tell me that returning as an adult might take away some of the fear."

"They have a point."

She rolled her eyes. "I don't want to go back."

"You think being there will make you relive it all over again."

Her head bobbed up and down.

"But you're stuck experiencing it all again and again anyway."

Her pale blue orbs glanced away before she said, "I am. So I should face it. Why have I waited all these years to realize that?"

"Trauma wraps each person in its own special web."

She dropped her arms to her lap. "What happens if you find the papers I told you about and they don't help with your search for the Clachers?"

"I continue helping you. My aid in this isna contingent on anything with the Clachers. If anything, that's a bonus."

"I want you to feel as if you can walk away at any time," she said.

Cináed smiled at her. "I hope you feel the same."

"Then we're in agreement."

"So it seems."

She looked away, a soft smile about her lips. "I have to admit, I'm glad you found me."

"You're just glad you backed into me," he teased.

Her gaze jerked back to him as she laughed. "Never."

He saw her eyes go to the dog bed and her smile faded. Cináed was glad she'd had her dog with her that night so Gemma didn't have to suffer through all of it alone. It built a connection with dogs, one that helped her get through each day.

"Shall I bring Duke with us?"

That made her laugh again. Cináed liked the sound of it. It was raw and full, nothing held back. For someone who was so reserved, it was nice to see that when she did give in to the humor, she let it all out.

"I think I'll be fine. But thank you for the offer," she said.

Cináed shrugged. "Or you could just make believe I'm the dog."

Their gazes met, held. He recalled the feel of her small, soft hand in his, of how she hadn't hesitated to take it. It showed that she trusted him—a little.

"If it comes to that," she replied softly.

His blood heated just thinking about their brief contact. Gemma was beautiful. Her vulnerability and steel backbone fascinated him. She was a contradiction and somehow that made her a temptation he couldn't resist.

"So," he said and cleared his throat while trying to pull his mind away from wondering what it would be like to kiss her. "Would you be ready to go to the isle tomorrow?"

She raised her shoulders to her ears and dropped them. "Why put it off, right? Tell me what airline, and I'll book my flight."

"We'll be flying by chopper."

"Oh. Right. Then tell me how much I owe for my share."

He tried to hide his grin, but he couldn't help it. He liked that she didn't assume anything. She had lived on her own nearly her entire life, and she was used to doing everything herself.

"Actually, Dreagan has a helicopter that we'll be taking."

Her eyes widened. "I see. And let me guess, you know how to fly it."

"Of course."

"Of course," she mimicked with a laugh.

Bit by bit she was relaxing. The smiles came easier, the laughter louder. He likened her to a flower. With each petal unfurling, he got to see a different side of her. And he liked each and every one.

"Unless you'd rather go a different route," he offered.

She shook her head of ginger hair. "I've never been in a helicopter before. I'm looking forward to it."

"I promise I'm a good pilot."

She cut her eyes to the messenger bag. "Not that I particularly want to discuss my past, but it is the reason you came. There is a small stack that I set aside."

Cináed opened the bag and pulled out each group of papers that had been clipped together. He set them all before her and watched while she shuffled through them until she came to the stack she'd mentioned.

Gemma handed it to him. "The authorities said that there were no witnesses to anything."

Cináed glanced at the paper before him. He remembered it. There was an account by a man who claimed that he saw a bright flash on the isle the night Gemma's family disappeared. The man told two different reporters, who wrote up pieces a year apart.

"Based on the police reports I read, no one questioned this man," Cináed told her.

She clasped her hands together on the table. "No, they didn't. But I did."

Now that surprised him. "And?"

"He has dementia and recalls nothing."

"I might send Merrill to talk to him. Perhaps we'll get lucky and find out something."

She bit her lip and picked at her thumbnail, which was chipped in the corner. "I never saw a bright light of any kind."

"It might be nothing more than lightning he saw. Then again, it could be something else. I doona like how the authorities didna talk to him."

Gemma leaned forward on the table and caught his gaze. "Based on everything you've read, do you think it was an accident like others say? That the rope holding the boat broke and slammed them up against the rocks?"

"It's a possibility, but I think if that were the case, then some evidence, whether bodies or bits of the boat, would have washed up on shore somewhere. There are too many isles in the Hebrides for there to be nothing."

"And what about the other theory? That my parents left me?"

Her voice was soft, a long-held fear finding its way into her words. He knew with 99.9 percent certainty the theory was false. Ryder was doing a secondary search for anyone matching the descriptions of Daniel, Laura, and Kyle Atherton since the night they went missing.

Cináed covered her hands with his. "You told me how desperately your mum wanted you on that boat. Your brother shouted for you. Your mum offered the locket. I doona believe they left you."

"Then where are they?" she asked, her forehead creasing.

"We'll get you an answer. You may no' like it though."

She shrugged and shook her head. "I need closure. It's the not knowing that has been the slowest death imaginable."

"Aye," he murmured, thinking about his dragons.

She shifted her hands and wrapped hers around his. "What did you lose?"

Just as Cináed was about to shrug off her words, he found himself saying, "Something verra important. I had to send them away to protect them."

"Them?" she asked.

It was the sorrow in her blue eyes that struck him right in the chest. There were few times he had spoken to any of the other Kings about the ache that stayed with him constantly for his clan. All the Kings missed their dragons. There was no need to talk about it.

But that wasn't the case with Gemma.

"It was the hardest decision to make," he told her. "But I had to give them a chance. I doona know where they are or if they're even alive."

"Can you not find out?"

Cináed's thoughts went to V. The King of Coppers was gifted with a sword that allowed him to not only check on the dragons, but to call them home when the time was right. Yet V had told them nothing of the dragons, and it was killing Cináed.

"There is a way, but it's tricky."

Gemma lifted one shoulder in a shrug. "I think it would be worth it."

"I doona agree. Right now, I believe they're alive and prospering. If V checks on them, I could find out that's exactly what is happening."

"Or you could discover they're hurting or dead," Gemma finished and twisted her lips in regret. "I'm sorry. I didn't think about that."

"I understand about wanting answers. I open my eyes every sunrise and hope that I get the ones I want."

Pale blue eyes lowered to their linked fingers. "Don't worry. I've prepared myself for the worst, just in case. I know what my odds are."

"There is much about this world you doona know," Cináed cautioned.

"Like what?" she asked, her head cocked to the side.

He briefly thought about telling her the truth about himself. Would she throw him out of her house and tell him he was crazy? Or would she believe him?

Cináed shook his head. "There are many unexplainable things."

"Are you talking aliens?" She sat back, pulling her hands from his. "I've watched enough Ancient Aliens to get where some people claim they've been here, and I'm not obtuse or ignorant to believe that we're the only beings in the universe. However, I don't think there are aliens among us."

He missed the feel of her immediately, but he didn't reach for her hand again. "Let me get this straight. You believe aliens are out there, but that they wouldna come here?"

"Precisely," she said with a nod. "Why would they want to come here? Look at us. As a species we're not exactly welcoming or willing to share. I believe they're steering clear of us."

"What about magic?"

She blinked at him. "You mean like magicians and stuff?"

"Some people claim they're Druids who can see into the future."

Gemma shook her head, but then she halted, a deep frown filling her brow. "Druids?"

Cináed studied her face. The word had struck something in her memories. He was sure of it. "That's right. They've been part of this continent for hundreds of years."

"My mother used to tell me a story about Druids." Gemma rose and put her hands on either side of her head. "How could I have forgotten something like that?"

He slowly got to his feet. "Do you happen to remember the story?"

Her arms dropped to her sides. Her eyes might be focused on him, but her mind was a million miles away. "There was something about a brother and sister. Kyle used to make fun of how much I loved the story. I would make Mum tell it to me every night."

"Was it from a book?"

Gemma blinked and came back to the present. "No, there wasn't a book. At least not one that I knew."

"How did the Druids fit in?"

"The siblings were Druids."

Cináed nodded. "We need to get to the isle as soon as possible."

"Now?"

"If you're up for it."

She shrugged. "What's a few hours? Now or in the morning?"

"How soon can you pack?"

Gemma took a step back. "Pack?"

"In case we have to stay overnight somewhere."

Her chest heaved, and he could see that she was debating on whether to go now that there was a chance they would stay on the isle. Then she blew out a breath.

"Give me fifteen minutes," she told him.

Chapter Twelve

It was really happening. She was going back.

The closer Cináed brought Gemma to the isle, the harder it became to breathe. The helicopter—a luxury one with all the amenities, because why not?—ate up the miles entirely too fast.

She sat in the front with him. Gemma was beginning to think it was so he could keep an eye on her. His frequent glances in her direction told her that she wasn't doing a good job of hiding the fact that she was actually considering jumping out of the chopper instead of returning to the place of her nightmares.

At first, the flight had been amazing. She had flown in planes before, but a helicopter gave another aspect entirely. Her eyes drank in the beauty, marveling at the landscape that she had never witnessed from such an angle.

Then the land gave way to water and a cold hand of terror wrapped around her heart, squeezing it until she couldn't catch her breath. She tried to close her eyes, but her lids wouldn't remain down. They popped open, trained on the horizon, waiting breathlessly for the sight of her old home.

"We can turn around."

Cináed's voice came through the headphones that helped dim the loud hum of the whirling blades. She turned her head and met his gaze. He was giving her a way out, allowing her to return to the safety of her world where she had effectively become a hermit.

Except, she couldn't do that. As much as she longed for it, she knew that he'd been right earlier. That night played in her mind constantly. It didn't matter whether she was on the isle or a million miles away. There was no escaping it. She'd tried for years.

She didn't consider herself particularly courageous. In fact, the way she'd lived proved just how cowardly she truly was. She might have continued on that course, but then Cináed had arrived and given her the locket.

Whether it was the sight of the necklace, Cináed, or visiting Dreagan and seeing the lengths he had gone through to look into her past, Gemma knew she couldn't bury her head in the sand anymore. A line had been drawn, and it was time she took a stand.

For herself. For her sanity.

For her future.

"Gemma?"

She couldn't see his eyes because of the sunglasses, but she knew they were trained on her. He waited patiently for her to make a decision. The little girl inside her screamed to retreat to the cottage and forget that any of this had even happened.

But the woman in her didn't want to run. She might shake and tremble and inwardly shout and cry, but she stood tall. For now, at least.

"Keep going," she told Cináed.

He bowed his head and returned his attention to the front. Gemma continued to stare at his profile. She had the impression that Cináed was genuinely interested in helping her. She hoped she wasn't wrong, because if he turned out to be a...she searched her mind for some analogy and kept coming back to a prince and frog.

It was a pretty decent parallel. Cináed, for all intents and purposes, was a prince. Gemma just hoped he remained that way. Because if he did turn out to be a frog, she might never again open herself up to anyone.

Without looking her way, Cináed reached over and touched her hand. It was a reassuring gesture, his way of telling her that he knew she was having a difficult time and he was there for her.

Gemma almost snorted out loud. No one had been there for her. Not once. The police, therapists, doctors, and anyone else who was able to get near her told her they wanted to help, but they lacked something in their eyes that gave her the assurance that they actually *would* help.

Whatever she'd searched for in others' eyes she found in Cináed's. As strange as that sounded. The odds had been stacked against her for as long as she could remember. And yet, somehow, Cináed had walked into her life and given her the little shake she had needed.

She only hoped that she could actually go through with what was about to happen. Would she be brave enough to stand on the isle and look at the spot she had last seen her family? Could she walk into the house and relieve the happy memories—as well as the worst?

"You can do this," Cináed said, as if reading her mind.

Gemma blinked and looked out the front of the chopper. Numerous isles—large and small—dotted the dark blue waters. The first years of her life had been spent in bliss upon the isle with no one other than her parents and brother for company. She hadn't thought it unusual since it was all she'd known. The times they had gone for supplies had been trips of joy and wonder, but she had always been happy to be back on their isle.

The chopper tilted as Cináed turned it. Gemma looked out the side, her eyes fastening on the remains of her old home. It looked as if it were barely holding itself together. And somehow that made her sad. Her once happy home looked depressed and desolate.

Cináed circled the isle twice. Gemma knew he was giving her time to take it in before landing. He also gave her a chance to decide if she could go through with it.

She looked at him and nodded before returning her attention to the isle. As he began to land the helicopter, she noted how green the grass was compared to the vibrant blue of the water. The tall grass swayed with the winds that swept across the barren isle. There wasn't a single tree upon it. Only piles of rocks, boulders jutting out of the earth and protruding into the turbulent sea.

And yet, her parents had decided to inhabit the tiny block of land.

Gemma spotted the beach on the east side of the isle closest to the Scottish coast. She and Kyle had played for hours in the surf. It had been one of her favorite spots.

All too soon, she lost sight of the beach as they descended and softly landed. With a few switches, Cináed shut off the engines. She didn't move, even when he removed his headphones and hung them up above him.

He took off his sunglasses and smiled at her. "How are you doing?"

"Fine," she said.

He raised a brow and glanced downward. Curious as to what he looked at, Gemma followed his line of sight to see her hands gripping the sides of the seat as if it were the only thing keeping her alive.

She made her fingers loosen. The ache that assaulted her let her know that she had been clutching the seat for quite some time.

Cináed said something but his voice was muffled, making it difficult to hear him. She shook her head, hoping he might repeat it. Then he reached over and removed her headphones.

Time and again she found herself doing stupid things around him. Would it ever end?

After he hung the headphones up and returned his gaze to her, he gave her a heart-stopping smile. "I said, you can do this."

"I thought I could. Now I'm not so sure."

"I'm here to help."

She hesitated, not sure what to do.

He unfastened his seatbelt and looked forward. "You've done everything on your own for so long that you believe you have to continue doing that. You can do this on your own. I believe you can do anything you want all by yourself." His head turned to her. "Asking for help doesna make you weak. Just the opposite, actually."

"How?" she asked.

"It means that you recognize two things. You have someone you know will be there for you, and that while you're capable of handling whatever it is, you choose no' to."

The way his gray eyes held hers, relaxed and unruffled, helped Gemma take her first easy breath since she'd climbed into the luxury chopper.

"Look at what you've accomplished," Cináed continued. "What you went through would have broken lesser people. Yet you no' only survived, you thrived. You made your own way in the world, figured out what you loved to do and made a career out of it. You stood on your own against the world. If you can do that, you can do anything."

Tears stung her eyes, and she had to look away lest she begin crying. "No one has ever said anything like that to me before."

"Someone should have told you that every day of your life."

She took a deep breath before she unbuckled the harness holding her into the seat. Her hand was on the handle of the door, but she couldn't quite make herself open it. She then slid her gaze to Cináed.

"I'll be right there," he told her before he exited the helicopter and walked to her side.

He opened the door and held out his hand. Gemma slid her palms against his. A calmness stole over her as soon as his fingers wrapped around hers. She didn't hesitate to climb out of the chopper.

The moment her feet met the ground, a shiver went through her.

But she didn't rush back into the helicopter. Instead, she stood strong. Because she had Cináed by her side.

He gave her a smile of encouragement. "I told you that you could do it."

"Standing here is different than walking around."

"It just takes one step at a time. You've been doing that your entire life."

Gemma lifted her face as the sea breeze ran over her. No matter how many times she had gone to the coasts and lochs around Scotland, there wasn't a place that could smell as heavenly as this isle. No matter the season, she had known only absolute happiness until that fateful night.

"Life was good here," she told Cináed. "Very good. So much laughter."

"Hold tight to those memories. You're going to need them."

She swallowed and swung her gaze to him. "Where do we go first?"

"That's your decision. You take me where you want to go."

Without hesitation, she walked toward the beach. True to his word, Cináed remained beside her, never letting go of her hand. Gemma blinked against the sun that went in and out of the clouds drifting past.

They had left the storms behind at Dreagan, which was exactly where she hoped they remained while she was on the isle.

When they reached the beach, a smile pulled at her lips. "I learned to swim here. This stretch of white sand was just another portion of what I considered paradise."

"It's a verra beautiful place," he murmured in agreement.

As much as she wanted to remain right there, she knew she couldn't. Gemma turned and faced the buildings. The one in the middle was the house where she'd been born. It looked even worse from the ground.

"The house has fallen into complete disrepair. Da would've hated that," she said.

"The isle is yours. You could have it repaired anytime you want."

His words made her frown. "Mine?"

"Did you no' realize?"

She shook her head, shrugging. "If anyone told me, I don't remember. So this is all...mine?"

"Aye."

"Oh."

He rubbed his thumb on the back of her hand. "Shall we walk to the house?"

Gemma moved closer to Cináed. Now that she had taken the help he offered, she leaned on him more and more. It was a foreign experience to be supported by someone else, but she had to admit that it felt nice.

"Yes," she said. "It's time I went back inside the house."

Chapter Thirteen

Cináed was rather impressed with how well Gemma was doing. Being on the isle was having a huge impact on her. She gripped his hand with the force of ten men, but it was the troubled look that filled her eyes that he wished he could erase.

But only she could do that by facing her past.

They walked to the house. Her steps were slow, hesitant even. He didn't rush her, letting her set the pace. He continued to see if any spells or wards could be found while Merrill searched in the water. Even though the two of them had already been to the isle, this time Gemma was with them.

When he and Gemma finally reached the residence, she stopped at the front door and touched the ivy that trailed from the lattice structure they walked beneath.

"Da wanted roses," Gemma said, looking up at the plant. "It was Mum who preferred ivy. She loved it. And Da gave her everything that she loved. At one time, there was ivy everywhere."

"It certainly has flourished here," Cináed pointed out.

Her fingers released the runner as her arm dropped to her side. "I used to try and jump up to reach it every time I came into the house."

Gemma focused on the door, which allowed Cináed to look around for some sign of Merrill, who had decided to travel by water. Merrill chose to follow some of the currents around the isle to see if he could find anything else at the bottom of the sea.

The door creaked loudly when Gemma pushed it open. It was so warped that it didn't shut properly. He tightened his hand around hers, and she gave him a grateful look before she stepped over the threshold.

Cináed had recently been there, so he kept his attention on her.

Minute emotions ran over her face. Shock at the state of things, bitterness at having her life stripped from her, and the pain of remembering that horrible night.

But it was the thread of terror that really caught his interest.

Just as he suspected, there was more to the story of that night than she had shared. If only she were willing to reveal more, he might be able to tell her exactly what happened. Because the more he listened to her and the more he walked the isle, the more he began to suspect that magic had been at work.

But magic from who? It wasn't the Dragon Kings, which left Druids or Fae. Coupled with the story that Gemma said her mother told her of two Druid siblings, which was eerily similar to the Clacher family who always had a brother and sister charged with regulating the Druids. Such coincidences just didn't happen.

Gemma swallowed heavily as she walked room by room on the first floor. She came to the stairs, and it took her several minutes before she put one foot on the bottom step and began to make her way up.

To his surprise, she bypassed the second floor and went straight to the attic. The stairs narrowed considerably, and the door was so short that he had to duck to get inside. With the decay of the roof, the contents of the attic had been exposed to the elements.

"There," Gemma said, pointing to the wardrobe that lay partially on its side now.

He started to walk to it and realized that she still had a hold of his hand. Cináed caught her gaze. "Would you rather stay here while I go look?"

"Yes," she said with a quick nod.

Despite her words, it took her another few moments before she loosened her fingers and released him. Cináed then walked to the piece of furniture and looked behind it.

"It looks like the wardrobe managed to shield the boxes from most of the rain, though the damp has set in for sure," he told her.

There were three boxes just as she'd said. He decided not to look through the boxes there. Instead, he opted to carry them to the helicopter. Except when he lifted one, the bottom fell out.

"Shite," he mumbled.

Behind him, Gemma giggled. "That's the sort of thing that usually happens to me."

He shot her a grin over his shoulder. Despite the mess, he was happy that she was able to find a little bit of humor. "You must be rubbing off on me."

"I hope so," she teased.

Cináed straightened and dusted off his hands. "I thought we might bring some things back with us. I have plastic containers in the chopper. I'll run out and get them."

Her lips parted as terror filled her gaze, but whatever she was about to say died on her lips. She clasped her hands together. "Do you need my help?"

"If you'd like to." He knew she probably wasn't keen on remaining in the house alone.

"I'll be fine," she stated after a small pause.

He gave her a nod. "I'll hurry."

Cináed rushed down the stairs and ran to the helicopter. As he neared it, he saw something out of the corner of his eye and turned to find an orange dragon head staring at him. He motioned Merrill back down into the water. It would just be their luck that someone from a neighboring isle would see a dragon head break the surface.

Or worse, Gemma.

As terrified as she was, Cináed didn't think she could ever find out about what he was. There were some humans who could handle it, but most couldn't. Unfortunately, Gemma fell into the latter category. And that really disappointed him. Not that he blamed her. She had been through something horrendous at a young age that prevented her from accepting anything normal, much less anything that couldn't be explained.

He got the plastic bins and rushed back to the house. When he walked into the attic, Gemma was in the same spot he'd left her. He didn't expect her to help him put the items in the boxes, but to his surprise, she did.

They did the chore silently and quickly. When it was finished, he carried two of the bins while she took the last one down the stairs. Cináed was outside before he realized that Gemma was no longer with him.

He dropped the tubs and went back inside, where he found her staring at a corner in the living room behind a chair. The sight of her so pale worried him. He gently took the tub from her hand and set it aside before he grasped her hands and stepped in front of her. She blinked a few times and focused on his face.

"Are you all right?"

She shook her head. "Have you ever thought you recalled everything about a moment in time? Then you return to the scene and realize that there is much you don't remember?"

"I've no'. Is that what happened?"

She looked around him and jerked her chin to the corner. "That's where I sat with Daisy until noon the next day. I don't remember the space being so small."

"It was a long time ago, and you had been through something horrible. Of course you willna recall every detail."

"I remember every strike of lightning as it struck the earth and lit up this room. I remember huddling into the tiniest ball so I wouldn't be seen. I remember the way Daisy shook as she pressed me against the corner. I remember the way my wet clothes suctioned to me and the cold seeped into my bones."

Cináed didn't interrupt her, even though she'd revealed a crucial clue. She had been hiding from someone. He didn't say anything about that or the wet clothes for the moment. While he expected her to have gotten soggy, there was something about the way she talked about wet clothes that made him think it was more than just rain that had been to blame.

Her blue eyes flashed angrily even as she linked her fingers with his. "How could I recall those details but not the space itself?"

"You can no' expect to recollect every detail from such a trauma. Some will always stick out more than others."

"If I forgot something like that, what makes you think I haven't forgotten something else? Or worse, misremembered something?"

He wondered if she knew that as she spoke, she walked closer to him, bridging the short gap between them. Cináed saw the silver flecks in her eyes. He wanted so badly to wrap an arm around her and pull her near, molding her body against his.

"I was so sure of things," she continued. "Now I'm doubting all of it."

When a single tear ran down her face, his control snapped. Cináed's arms went around her. She pressed her cheek against his chest and clung to him.

"Then it's time you found out the truth," he whispered against her hair.

She sniffed loudly. "In order for that to happen, you need to know the rest of the story."

He leaned back and cupped her face between his hands. "What you're doing takes more courage than most people manage in a lifetime."

To his shock, she leaned forward and pressed her mouth against his. They remained still, locked in time as if both were afraid to move.

Her soft lips against his brought his already heated blood to a boil. Just when he shifted to get a better angle for another kiss, Gemma pulled back. Her tongue glided over her lower lip like she was tasting him.

His cock jumped, begging him to taste more of her.

"I'm sorry for that," she began.

He slid his hands through her cool length of ginger hair. "Doona apologize for kissing me. Ever."

"Really?"

"Really."

She blew out a breath and stepped back, but she trailed her hands down his arms to his hands. "I don't normally like people touching me, but it's different with you. When you're touching me, I want more."

Damn. She really needed to stop, because if she didn't, Cináed wasn't sure what he was going to do. Kiss her for sure, but it wouldn't stop there.

"Then I willna stop," he promised.

Her lips curved into a smile. They said no more as they took the tubs to the chopper.

"Will you walk with me to the dock?" she asked.

"Of course."

They made their way hand in hand from the house and down to the quay. Gemma stood on the remains of the wooden dock. Cináed spotted Merrill beneath the surface, but Merrill made sure not to get close enough for Gemma to see him.

"My life was idyllic," she said. "Nothing of the world touched us. Not even the little time we spent in the villages to get supplies. Looking back, I can say it's like we were cocooned in some bubble that kept others away."

Cináed frowned, because her words made him think of the bubble of magic around MacLeod Castle that kept the warriors and Druids from being found by the outside world.

"That's why I fought so hard not to leave." Gemma glanced at him, shrugging. "I knew something was wrong, even that young. After I got my dog and returned to this spot, the boat was gone."

He jerked his gaze to hers. "Gone?"

"The light was out, but the lightning flashed enough that I could see that the boat was no longer docked. At first, I thought my parents left me. Then I felt it."

A shudder went through her so forcefully that he turned and pulled her against him. Gemma placed one of her hands on his chest but her eyes never left the water.

"I couldn't see what it was, but I knew it was there. Daisy barked at everything, but all she did was whine this time. It felt like someone had poured ice in my veins I was so terrified. I ran. There."

He looked in the direction she pointed along the rocky edge, wondering how the waves hadn't taken her over the side.

She inched closer to him. "The waves were so high and the rain came down so hard that it was difficult to see anything. A wave knocked me on my knees, and Daisy slipped from my hands. Then the next thing I knew, I was in the water."

Cináed's heart clutched. He knew the force of such storms. There was no way she should have survived.

"Before the water took me, I saw the form," she continued. "The waves dragged me down so deep I didn't think I'd get back up. When I started swimming, I stopped just before I reached the surface because I knew whatever was on the isle waited for me to come up for air. I remained in the water despite my lungs burning until I could take it no more. When my head breached, I was relieved to find I was alone.

"Daisy was waiting for me. I got her and went to the back of the house where I knew one of the windows wasn't latched. I snuck in and huddled in the corner with my dog while the person walked through my house."

Cináed had so many questions, but he asked just one. "Did you see who it was?"

"All I saw was a dark silhouette against the night. I don't know if it was a man or a woman."

"But you felt something?"

She nodded. "Evil."

He rubbed a hand up and down her back and looked at the water slamming against the rocks. And it was a calm day. It was a pure miracle that she had survived.

Chapter Fourteen

There had been a time Gemma knew without a doubt that someone had been on the isle with her the night her family disappeared. Then, later, she began to question herself. So many told her that she had been a child and couldn't possibly have grasped the entire situation as an adult would. Because, otherwise, she would be able to tell them what happened to her parents and brother.

That's when she began to doubt what she remembered. That's when she wondered if the figure had been a figment of her imagination.

Now, after being on the isle and standing at the dock, the memories had risen up like a tidal wave, swarming Gemma with the truth. She hadn't been alone. She knew it for a certainty. It also helped tremendously that Cináed hadn't hesitated in believing her.

"Did the entity say anything to you?" Cináed asked. "Did they make any kind of noise?"

She shook her head. "If they did, I didn't hear it over the sound of the storm."

"Did you see them do anything?"

"No. I wouldn't have seen their silhouette if it hadn't been for the lightning."

"But they saw you."

She swallowed, unable to hold back a shiver as she recalled how it felt to have the attention of such a...*thing*...on her. "Without a doubt. If I had surfaced from the water while it stood on the rocks, I wouldn't be here talking to you."

"Nay, I doona think you would."

Gemma watched as Cináed's gray eyes slid to the water, his forehead furrowed deep in thought for several minutes.

"What are you thinking?" she asked, unable to hold back her curiosity.

"I'm still mulling that over."

"You know something you aren't telling me."

Cináed sighed and turned his head to her. There was a deep resolve in his gaze that warned her that he was keeping many things from her. Yet, for some reason she didn't get the feeling that he was trying to take advantage or harm her.

Instead...she thought he might be protecting her.

"Tell me," she urged.

He gave a single shake of his head. "I doona think it's time."

"What does that mean?"

"It means that you are no' ready."

She looked at him, searching his face. "I came back here. It was the last place I want to be. I'm ready."

Without thinking, she reached for his hand. She didn't know why she had the inescapable urge to not only stand next to Cináed, but to have a hold of him, as well. She knew it didn't make sense, and while she told herself to step back and release him—she couldn't.

Cináed glanced down at their hands before his eyes returned to her face. His free hand rose and he slid his fingers along her neck and into her hair, gently holding her.

Her heart hammered in her chest. Not from fear, but from desire. There was no denying what it was. It rose swiftly, consuming her. And she welcomed it.

Embraced it.

As she sank into his eyes, she realized why she gravitated toward him. She felt safe with Cináed. The passion she felt, however, was another matter entirely. It was what recklessly propelled her to kiss him earlier.

And, oh, what a kiss.

Just a soft press of their lips together, but it had been glorious. She wanted more. It was all she could think about now as he held her against him. Their bodies were touching. She didn't remember moving but that didn't matter when she was drowning in the beautiful gray pools of his eyes.

Her lids slid shut when his head lowered toward her. A heartbeat later, his lips were on hers. She released a breath she hadn't realized she'd been holding. And before she could grasp that he had kissed her, his mouth was moving over hers. With each touch of their lips, she was falling further and further under the desire that ruled her.

Then he let out a soft sigh and glided his tongue along her lips. She parted her mouth so their tongues could tangle and dance together.

Her heart leapt, her blood sizzled. And her body pulsed with a need she had never felt before.

The soft kiss quickly turned heated as their arms wrapped around each other. His hands traveled down her back before he palmed her butt. Then he pressed her against him and she felt the evidence of his arousal.

Excitement tore through her. The moment she moaned in response, Cináed deepened the kiss, taking her breath away. It all felt so good that she could have stood there for eternity and kissed him. Time was forgotten as she tumbled deeper into the passion that had them firmly in its grip.

It was the raindrop that pulled her to the present.

She ended the kiss and looked up. Dark clouds were moving toward them.

"Gemma, look at me," Cináed said.

She had to force her eyes away from the sky.

He held her gaze a moment. "It's going to be all right. I'm right here with you. It's just a little rain."

"I can't stay here," she told him.

Cináed took her hand and led her to the helicopter. He made sure she was secure before hurrying to his side and starting the blades while he buckled himself in.

She couldn't seem to stop watching the way one fat drop at a time landed upon the front window. Thankfully, they were up in the air and flying away not long after. Cináed didn't take them far.

Gemma recognized Skye even from the air. She had been on the isle a few times herself. There was a particular look about Skye that made it easy for her to pick out. The farther that Cináed took her from her isle, the more she relaxed.

They flew over Skye, and she took in the rugged beauty of the mountains and glens. She spotted a cottage sitting alone between a river and the base of a mountain. When she realized they were descending, she jerked her head to Cináed.

He just grinned at her.

Sure enough, he set the chopper down near the white-washed

cottage. Gemma kept waiting for someone to come out and greet them, but no one stirred from within.

She climbed out of the helicopter and waited for Cináed. Then she asked, "Whose place is this?"

"It's one of many properties Dreagan owns," he explained.

Her brows shot up in her head. "Here? Why?"

"Why no'?" was his response.

When he took her hand and gave her a tug, she dug in her heels. Gemma shook her head when he looked at her. "That isn't an explanation."

Cináed blew out a breath. "The short answer is that we do have property all over the world. Some small cottages like this, others huge mansions like in Venice."

"Italy?" she asked, then realized how stupid that was.

"Aye. We like to make sure that there is a place for us to stay when we travel."

"You never stay in hotels?"

He lifted one shoulder in a shrug. "I wouldna say never. It does happen."

"Why here on Skye? Why this place?"

"It's beautiful, for one," he said as he looked at the cottage.

When he didn't continue, she quirked a brow in question. "And the second reason?"

"Dreagan has an interest in some of those here on Skye."

Gemma frowned, noting that he had chosen his words carefully. "What do you mean?"

"I'm no' sure you're ready to hear this."

"Please," she urged.

Cináed rubbed his jaw as he turned his head away from her. He gazed at the river flowing past for a few moments. Then he returned his attention to her. "Skye is home to some of the most powerful Druids in the world."

She waited for him to laugh or show some sign that he was joking. When he didn't, she realized that he was very serious. "Druids? Like...Druids?"

A ghost of a grin played upon his lips. "Exactly like that."

"So they're like some cult or something?"

The smile vanished. "Nay. They have magic. Real magic. Maybe it would've been better if I brought you to them instead of trying to explain it."

Her brain heard his words, but she was having a difficult time processing what he said.

Cináed sighed loudly. "I told you it was too soon for you to know."

"It's not," she replied.

He gave her a dubious look. "I beg to differ."

"You believe in magic?"

"I do."

The way he said the words, without any hesitation or laughter, made her wonder if he spoke the truth. She hadn't doubted Cináed since they'd agreed to work together, and she didn't like that she was doing it now.

"I'm no' lying," he told her.

She shrugged, not knowing what else to do. "I've never seen magic."

"I can show you."

"You?" The word came out like a screech, which she instantly regretted.

Cináed chuckled. "Aye, me."

"You have...magic?" Did she actually just ask that question?

It seemed so...odd. It certainly wasn't something she'd ever imagined herself asking anyone.

"I do."

"Show me."

He pressed his lips together briefly, hesitating.

"Please." Suddenly she really wanted to see Cináed do magic. "I want to see."

"Gemma," he began.

She quickly interrupted him. "I told you everything about that night. Something I've never shared with another soul. You know my secret. I'm now asking you to tell me yours."

He jerked back slightly.

The action proved to her that Cináed did have a secret. And a whopper by his reaction. But she set that aside and continued talking. "You're the one who brought up magic. If you can do it, then I want to see."

"But you doona believe."

"Prove me wrong," she challenged.

He searched her eyes for a long moment. "It was a mistake to say anything to you."

"Maybe, but the words have already been spoken. You can't take them back. Do you believe that I can't handle it?"

Cináed shook his head. "I doona believe your mind is open to such things yet."

"I guess we're about to find out, aren't we?" She crossed her arms over her chest and waited.

He glanced away, shaking his head again, this time more to himself. "Doona say I didna warn you," he cautioned.

Gemma didn't reply, just waited.

Cináed took a deep breath and held out his hand. At first she didn't see anything. Then she saw it—a pinpoint of green that grew into a seed that soon sprouted and a stem surged upward.

Her arms dropped to her sides when a bud formed. A second later, the petals opened to reveal a pale pink rose.

Before she realized it, Cináed held out the flower to her. Gemma took it without thinking. She winced when the pad of her finger touched a thorn. There was no doubt that she held a real rose, not some manipulation of light.

She looked from the flower to Cináed. "You can do magic."

Chapter Fifteen

Her surprise was obvious. Cináed watched Gemma carefully. She didn't look as if she were about to bolt, but she did look as if her world had been turned on its side.

He would've laughed at the entire scenario if it wasn't such a tangled situation. It was obvious that Gemma hadn't completely believed he could do magic. Everything could have gone to shite. Somehow, it hadn't.

Gemma hadn't taken her eyes from the rose. Cináed wasn't sure why he had chosen that color or flower. It just seemed to suit her.

"Roses are my favorite," she murmured.

"We should get inside before the weather reaches us."

She nodded absently and turned toward the cottage. Cináed made sure she stayed with him as he walked to the dwelling. As he approached, he unlocked the wards around the house that would let them in.

He opened the door and stepped aside, sweeping his arm to indicate she should enter. Gemma paused and frowned at the door. She looked from the door to him.

"You don't keep it locked?" she asked.

He shrugged. "Magic."

She said no more as she entered the house. While she spent a few minutes looking around the simple cottage, Cináed checked the wood stacked in the fireplace and found the matches.

He wasn't sure why he'd told her he could do magic. Maybe it was because he wanted her to know his secret. It was a huge chance he'd taken. She was barely holding things together as it was, and he'd just made things worse by showing off in front of her.

Because that's exactly what it had been. He wanted to be special in her eyes. He'd gotten his wish, but it was anyone's guess how this could turn out.

"Why not use magic?" she asked.

"I usually only do that when I have to. Occasionally, I'll use it for something like lighting fires."

"Like growing a rose?"

He looked up at her from his place squatting on the floor. "Something like that."

She had yet to set down the flower. Cináed was ready to tell her he would give her a rose every day if she wanted. Instead, he straightened and stood before her.

"Your perception of me has changed. I hope for the good."

Gemma shrugged. "You have an ability that I didn't know was even possible. Have you always been able to do magic?"

"Aye."

"Can everyone at Dreagan?"

He paused before shaking his head. "No' everyone."

"Are you a Druid?"

This was the one question he'd known was coming but hoped wouldn't. Despite realizing she would ask it, he hadn't come up with anything good to tell her.

"Cináed?"

He inwardly shook himself. "Nay, I'm no' a Druid."

"I see," she murmured. "So more than Druids have magic?"

"That's right."

She smiled ruefully. "This is where you tell me I'm not ready to learn the truth."

He opened his mouth to stop her when she turned away and went to the kitchen to look for something to use as a vase for the flower. Cináed walked out of the cottage to the chopper and began bringing in the tubs of files they'd taken from the attic.

With the weather coming soon, he should get set up so in case the rain turned into a thunderstorm, Gemma had something to take her mind off it.

He finished bringing all three in to find that she had searched the cupboards and fridge to find some cheese, crackers, and wine. She was looking for a wine opener when he reached around her and opened a drawer, pulling it out.

"Oh. Thanks," she said with a little laugh.

He set to opening the bottle while she searched for glasses. As he poured the wine, she pulled back the packaging on the cheese. Cináed then got a knife and began to cut it while she opened the cracker package. All of it was done in companionable silence, and yet he had the distinct impression that she was observing him.

"Hmm," she said after taking a bite of cheese. "This is really good."

"Wait until you try it with the wine."

She immediately did that and grinned as she nodded. "Very good."

The talk ceased. They each took a chair and stared at the table while eating. After a couple of crackers, Cináed reached for the first tub and began rifling through it. There were old documents involving the parents, such as bank statements and the like.

The second box yielded nothing, both of which he moved toward Gemma in case she wanted to search through them. Which she did.

It wasn't until Cináed opened the third bin and picked up a file that he realized he'd stumbled upon a treasure. Within the file were papers, disintegrating from age and exposure, outlining—in detail—the family lineage straight to the Clachers.

And at the bottom of the paper were two names: Kyle and Gemma.

Cináed lifted his gaze to Gemma. She did a double take when she realized he was staring.

"What is it?" she asked.

"Do you remember the document you saw that had the Clacher name?"

She shook her head, her lips twisting. "Not really."

"Was it this?" he asked turning the page to her.

Gemma leaned closer to read the faded writing better. It took her a moment to go through the lineage until she found her name.

Her gaze jerked to his. "What does this mean?"

"Exactly what I thought it might. You're a Clacher. It's been kept secret for generations, but someone was smart enough to keep a family history."

"I'm an Atherton. My father showed me the family history."

"And I would bet it matches this almost perfectly. The only difference is the names."

She sat back and took a long drink of wine. "You said the Clachers were wiped out."

"Everyone believed they were, but we might be wrong." He glanced at the rest of the tub and realized that the answers might very well lie within.

As if sensing the magnitude of possibilities, Gemma scooted her chair closer and exchanged a look with him. Then they both reached for a file.

It took another three hours where Gemma was so engrossed in the papers that she hadn't yet realized the rain was coming down steadily. For his part, Cináed was finding more and more documented proof that substantiated the claim that Gemma was indeed a Clacher.

The only thing left to find was how some Clachers had managed to survive the attack on Eigg that had taken the rest of those who bore the name.

"Oh," Gemma said.

Cináed glanced over to what she had found. The journal was literally falling apart, and she carefully turned the pages. He held his hands above it and spelled it to keep the journal intact.

"Thank you," Gemma said.

He flashed her a smile and leaned over her shoulder to read. It appeared to be a journal by someone named Keavy detailing her very ordinary life—as a Druid. She spoke of ceremonies and everyday life with magic.

It went on to detail the very difficult birth of her son. But it was the next passage that excited Cináed.

The family holds a great honor. Some Druids fear us, but most understand that our duty is to protect the humans who encounter Druids and are harmed, whether intentionally or not.

I think it's a blessing that every Clacher has a son and a daughter, which allows the continued patrolling of the Druids. We're so far down the line that I doubt my children (if I'm able to have a second) will ever be part of the powerful brother-sister duos who bring such balance to our world, but I can hope.

"I knew it," Cináed said.

Gemma looked at him. "What? Did you find what you were looking for?"

"I did," he said with a smile. He then got the family tree and pointed to a name toward the top of the document before he flipped to the front of the journal to show the name again.

"It's the same woman."

Cináed nodded. "She came from Eigg, which means she was a Clacher there. If we're lucky then she documented how she managed to escape."

Gemma flipped through the rest of the journal until Cináed glimpsed something on a page. He halted her and turned back to what had caught his attention.

"There," he said.

Gemma read it aloud. "The impossible has happened. Our beautiful haven has been attacked. Despite the power and influence of our family, no one came to help. We were decimated so quickly. The screams will remain with me forever. I watched my husband and family killed one by one. If it hadn't been for my husband, my son and I would have been lying on the ground next to him. But he took me to a secret entrance to the caves we found when we were teenagers.

"I didn't want to go. It was so slippery. I feared that I would fall and harm my son. With the cries of the dying and the shrieks of the yellow monsters who attacked us, I put one foot in front of the other. I didn't dare use any magic since the creatures seemed to home in on that. Despite everything, I managed to make it to the sea with my child. There waited a rowboat.

"I wanted as far from the carnage as I could get—after all, I wished my son spared from such a death—but I waited in the caves until nightfall. When I thought it might be safe, I heard the monsters over the crash of waves and knew we couldn't leave yet. For three days I stayed in the caves with my child. It was then that I finally climbed in the boat. Then I rowed. I had no direction, just away from Eigg.

"It felt as if I rowed for eternity before I finally came onto shore. I had no idea why Eigg had been targeted, but just to be safe, I told no one I was a Clacher. I changed mine and my son's surname to Atherton. The Clacher name would remain a secret until we could once again claim our rightful destiny."

Gemma finished and looked up at him. "What does that mean?"

Cináed ran a hand down his face. "It means she got verra lucky. It also means that story your mother told you about the brother and sister who policed Druids was her way of handing down your heritage."

"Why not just tell me?"

"You were a child."

Gemma glanced out the window. "They went to such lengths to

hide the Clacher name. And I took it."

"It doesna seem to have had any kind of negative effect."

"Is all this why my parents kept us on the isle away from everyone?"

Cináed lifted one shoulder. "It could be."

"If it was safe to use the Clacher name, why wouldn't they have? Why wouldn't they claim their heritage?"

"Your heritage," he corrected. "And perhaps it had been too long."

Gemma shook her head. "What happened to my parents, it has to do with this. I know it."

Cináed had believed that for a while, but he didn't want to scare her. "It might, but I doona think you're in danger. Look how long you've carried the Clacher name."

"Years," she said.

"Has anyone come for you?"

She shook her head of ginger hair.

Cináed smiled. "Then there you have it."

"I'm part of a world of magic. Of Druids," she added. "And I know nothing about them. It's all part of the answers I've been looking for. Will you tell me what I seek?"

"Aye."

Her smile was blinding. "All of it. Don't hold anything back. I can take it. I did fine with the flower."

Cináed grinned slightly. "There is a lot more to the story. You need to prepare yourself."

"I'm not scared. Not with you," she confessed.

He held out his hand and she took it. The moment their palms touched, his eyes softened. "You trust me?"

"I do."

Her words touched him deeply. He pulled her up and into his lap, where he feasted upon her lips.

Chapter Sixteen

She could kiss him all day. Gemma loved the way Cináed's mouth moved over hers. It was equal parts tender and demanding, soft and unrelenting. With just a kiss he could take her breath away. Her knees grew weak and her body became his to do with as he wanted.

Oh, the things she wanted him to do.

Gemma threaded her fingers through the short strands of his hair at the back of his neck. His moan made her breathing quicken. She wanted to be the one to bring that sound from him. She wanted to have him craving her as she did him.

Suddenly his mouth was gone and she was lifted in the air. Then she found herself straddling him. Her hands automatically rested on his thick shoulders. She couldn't resist the feeling of the muscles moving beneath her palms. Her exploration took her down over his firm pecs.

All the while, his hands were doing exploring of their own. Down her back to her butt that he gripped tightly before grinding her against him.

She looked into his gray eyes and without a word, he easily busted through the walls she had erected. Being with him was effortless, as if it had always been meant to be.

Her lips parted on a sigh when his hands slowly ran up her back to tangle in her hair. Then he gently tugged on the length until she leaned her head back. Gemma moaned the moment his warm tongue slid along her skin. Then his lips were there.

She closed her eyes, lost in the pleasure. But it was just getting started.

One large hand supported her back while his other held firm in her hair, keeping her immobile as he licked and kissed one side of her neck to the other. Then his attention moved downward to her breasts.

Her hips undulated when his mouth skimmed over her nipple. Through her shirt and bra she felt the heat of his mouth. It ripped through her like a current straight to her sex, which clenched hungrily.

Cináed's fingers loosened in her hair and she lifted her head to find him gazing at her with desire that darkened his eyes to a stormy gray.

"I want you," she whispered.

The corners of his lips turned up, hinting at a smile. His hands cupped her butt as he stood. She clung to him, her heart beating rapidly at the thought of being in his arms.

Of having him inside her.

He carried her into the bedroom and stopped near the bed. There he kissed her and slowly lowered her legs until her feet were on the ground.

Then his arms were around her, holding her against him so tightly that they were nearly one. She heard the tapping of rain on the window, but she didn't care. Nothing mattered but being in Cináed's arms—and the pleasure he gave her.

His hands slipped beneath the hem of her shirt. The contact of his palm against her stomach made her jerk in surprise. He pulled back, but she grabbed his hand and ended the kiss to look at him.

"Don't stop," she told him.

Two words were all it took to have him smile seductively. She shivered, because she knew she was going to be putty in his hands—but it was going to be a glorious time.

Not wanting to wait, she removed her shirt and reached for his, but he was quicker. She had never gotten out of her boots and jeans so fast before. Her fingers fumbled with the fastening of her bra. It was Cináed who unhooked it. It was also Cináed who helped right her when she nearly tipped over trying to take off her panties.

She wanted to take her time looking him over, but the desire was too much for both of them. Gemma did manage to see more hard sinew that covered the rest of his body as well as a dusting of hair on his wide chest. Her gaze skidded to a stop when she saw the red and black ink of the dragon tattoo that ran down his left side from his ribs to his knee.

He gently turned her face to him. They were skin to skin again, their lips locked together as he turned her toward the bed. In one smooth movement, he had them both on the mattress. The feel of his weight atop her was amazing.

She ran her hands up his back, marveling that he was with her. She readied to explore his marvelous body—especially his arousal that she could feel against her. She'd been too intent on his chiseled abs to think about looking lower earlier.

Then he rolled them to the side while still kissing her deeply. His hand roamed over her hip and thigh. She lifted her leg, throwing it over his. They weren't near enough to suit her. She needed him closer. So much closer.

His hand moved between them to cup her breast. The moment he found her nipple, she groaned at the exquisite feeling as he rolled it between his fingers. Her hips rocked against him, searching for any kind of friction.

She quickly fell under the spell of desire he wove around her. And all she could think about was that she hoped the night never ended.

* * * *

She was glorious. Cináed couldn't take his eyes off her. From her heady kisses to the way she clung to him, everything she did made him long for her more.

And her body. Her smooth, alabaster skin flushed with desire made his balls tighten. He couldn't wait to run his hands from her pink-tipped breasts to the indent of her waist and then over the swells of her hips down to her sex.

Not wanting to spook her, Cináed had taken things slow. Right up until she told him not to stop. Now, he couldn't get to her fast enough.

The feel of her pert breast in his palm was amazing, but it didn't compare to the ecstasy that spread over her face when he teased her nipple.

Unable to resist any longer, he glided his hand down her beautiful body to the juncture of her thighs. The moment he neared, she spread her legs, granting him access.

Cináed's breathing intensified when he felt how wet she was. The moment he pushed a finger inside her, she tore her lips from his and moaned loudly. It was a heady experience to watch the pleasure moving through her.

He had to see more, to give her more. Cináed found her clit and swirled his finger around it. Gemma's quick intake of breath and the way her back arched made him ache to be inside her, to fill her deeply.

To claim her, to mark her.
To make her his.

* * * *

Nothing had ever felt so good. Gemma was swallowed by an abyss of pleasure. Every nerve ending in her body sizzled with awareness, aching and yearning for more of Cináed's touch.

While she drowned in the bliss of him tantalizing her clit, she found she was quickly and effortlessly flung toward an orgasm. There was no stopping it—or Cináed. He worked her body as if he knew exactly where to touch her to send her flailing helplessly amid the pool of pleasure.

Just when she thought it couldn't get any better, his tongue replaced his finger on her clit and that same finger filled her, thrusting in and out of her.

The climax rose swiftly, consuming her. Her body jerked from the sheer force of it, while her mouth parted on a cry that lodged in her throat. Her fingers clutched helplessly at the covers as she fought to grab hold of something, anything.

Cináed worked her body, extending the climax until she couldn't take any more. Then he rose up over her, spreading her legs wide with his.

Her eyes opened to look up at him. The satisfaction on his face made her body clench. He knew exactly what he'd done to her. And he was going to do it again.

Gemma reached for him. The moment she touched his skin, damp with sweat, she needed him inside her. "Please," she begged.

"You can have all of me," he told her.

She looked down as he grabbed his cock. Her eyes widened at the size of him, but she didn't have too long to stare because he rubbed the head of his rod against her before he entered her.

Gemma dug her nails into his sides as he gradually filled her. And once he was inside her, he began to move and she learned what true ecstasy was.

He buried himself deep and ground his hips against her. Then he pulled out until just the tip of him was inside her before thrusting hard.

She bit her lip, waiting to see where he would take them next. His magnificent body was a work of art, but it was the way he made love to her that truly set him apart from others.

He moved slowly, rocking his hips back and forth while staring down at her. Gradually, he increased his tempo until he plunged hard and fast. He lowered himself to his forearms, and she took advantage of that by kissing his neck and nipping at his earlobe.

When he groaned in response, she continued her assault while letting her hands roam over his back and incredible ass. She had never been so hot for anyone before. Never yearned to have anyone touch her as he did.

Never longed to be so connected to anyone.

Until Cináed.

He changed everything.

All thoughts ceased when Cináed stopped moving and said her name. She met his gaze, wondering at the seriousness in his gray eyes.

"This is only the beginning," he told her.

She smiled and nodded. "Yes."

And then he began pumping his hips. She buried her face in his neck, her eyes shut as her body became his. She loved the feel of him, of the way his body moved against hers. Of how their sweat-soaked skin slid against each other.

She locked her ankles around his waist and met each thrust. The world fell away, leaving just the two of them to experience the kind of pleasure that Gemma had only read about. She held him tighter, wondering how in the world she had gotten so lucky that he'd found her.

His hips pistoned faster until he stiffened, a low, ragged moan falling from his lips. Satisfaction filled her knowing that she had brought him to orgasm.

And she wanted to do it again.

Except she wanted to have her mouth on his cock, watching his face as she did.

They remained locked in each other's arms for several minutes. She wanted to know what he was thinking, but if she asked, he might want to know her own thoughts, and she wasn't sure she could put into words what she was feeling.

In a very short time she had met Cináed, agreed to work with him, opened up enough to tell him about her past, and trusted him to bring her to the isle. For someone who rarely spoke to anyone unless she didn't have a choice, these were huge steps.

And yet it all felt right. As if it was destined for this to happen. Like she was supposed to meet Cináed, and he was supposed to...she didn't know what, but she knew he was important. Somehow.

Cináed pulled out of her and rolled to his side. She didn't have to worry if he wanted her against him, because he tugged her until she was right alongside him, one leg thrown over his.

"That was amazing," he said and kissed her forehead.

Gemma smiled. "It sure was. Can we do it again?"

He chuckled and looked down at her. "Without a doubt we will."

She settled her cheek against him and sighed. "I haven't felt this relaxed in...well, I can't remember when."

"Good." His hand moved along her hair from her forehead back. "You deserve happiness."

"So do you."

"You make me happy."

She shifted her head to look at him. He took the opportunity to kiss her softly before tucking her head back on his chest.

"Cináed, tell me of the magical beings. I want to know."

Chapter Seventeen

Cináed couldn't deny her request. Gemma had a right to know all of it. Unfortunately, by revealing even the tiniest part of what was just out of sight from the majority of mortals, he wouldn't be able to keep the Dragon Kings out of it for long. If at all.

"Why are you afraid to tell me?" she asked. "If I'm going to accept who I really am, then shouldn't I know it all?"

"Aye."

She shifted her head to look at him. "I can handle whatever it is you tell me. Or is it that you believe I'll tell others?"

"Nay, I doona think that's it."

"Then what?"

Cináed sighed. "The world you live in, the one where no one has magic, isna the real one. It's the one that those of us with magic strive to maintain for you."

"That's silly. People either have magic or they don't. Why should those that do have to pretend?"

He quirked a brow. "Take a look around. You doona even have to go back far. Look at today's headlines. There is always someone pitted against someone else."

Her nose wrinkled as she flattened her lips. "Good point."

"Neither the Druids nor the Fae were the first magical beings on this realm," he began.

Gemma sat up, crossing her legs as she sat next to him. "Go on," she said eagerly.

"Humans were no' the first beings either."

Her eyes widened. "I never even considered that option. That's amazing. Who were the first?"

For all his dithering about being unsure of what, if anything, to tell her about the Dragon Kings, Cináed had cast it all aside and went in for it all.

"Dragons."

"Dragons?" she repeated. Then her gaze briefly looked down to his tattoo. Her fingers skimmed over the dragon that looked as if it were crawling up his side, wings tucked and tail trailing. "Every culture around the world has some kind of dragon myth. Now it makes sense. There have been no skeletons or sightings of dragons since. Well, except for that video hoax and movies. So where did the dragons go?"

"They were sent away. You see, there were millions of dragons that occupied this realm. All sizes and colors, or clans, as they were called. Each clan had a king. A Dragon King. He was the strongest with the most power, and he was chosen by the magic upon this earth."

"Amazing," she murmured, leaning forward, waiting to hear more.

"The dragons lived here for millions of generations, and then one day, mortals arrived. Dragons speak telepathically, making it impossible to talk to the humans. But then each King shifted out of their true form into that of a mortal."

Gemma smiled, her gaze locked on him. "That's how they were able to talk to the humans. Did they become friends?"

"For a time. The Kings each gave up a portion of their land so the mortals could make a life. They had no magic, so the Kings felt as if it was their duty to protect them. They made a vow to always defend the humans. And for a while, everyone lived in harmony. The mortals, however, reproduced at an astonishing rate. It wasna long before the Kings had to give up more land. As you can imagine, that didna go well with some of the dragons."

She snorted as her brow furrowed. "I know how humans would react if someone tried to do that to them, so I can imagine how the dragons felt."

"Despite all of this, the King of Dragon Kings fought to keep the balance between the two species calm. It didna help that every once in awhile a dragon would eat a mortal. It was even worse when the humans hunted the smaller dragons for food. There were mortals who sought to be near the Kings. Some Kings even lived among them."

Her pale blue eyes held his as she nodded. "If a King could shift into that of a human, then I'm assuming that a few found lovers among the mortals?"

"They did. But even that wasna easy. There were some humans who became pregnant, but they soon lost the babes. Only a couple ever carried the bairn to term, but it was stillborn."

Gemma shifted and put her hand atop his. "So there is no half dragon-half human walking around?"

"No. But that didna stop one King from falling in love and wanting to marry his mortal lover. Unbeknownst to him, she had conspired with his uncle to kill him."

Gemma jerked back, her eyes widening in shock. "Please tell me she didn't succeed."

"She never got close, but if she had, she would have learned that the only one who can kill a Dragon King is another Dragon King."

"I don't even know these beings, but that seems like a very unscrupulous thing to do. What happened to this woman?"

"Constantine, the King of Dragon Kings, discovered what she was about. He gathered all the Kings except the one in love with her, and they hunted her down, killing her. Her King was furious when he learned what had happened without him. He couldn't believe he was deceived in such a way, and he reacted by waging war on the mortals. His dragons, Silvers, were some of the biggest, and he took them and slaughtered thousands."

Gemma pulled her legs up to her chest and rested her chin on her knees. "He did that all by himself?"

"Other Kings joined him. The mortals had pushed them to such an extent that they no longer cared about the vow they'd made when the humans first arrived. They just wanted their lives back to the way they had been."

"The dragons had magic."

"And they could fly, as well as breathe fire," he added.

She shook her head. "Then tell me how there are humans still walking around but no dragons?"

"Because Constantine stepped in. He was the type to honor a vow, regardless of how his feelings might have changed. It took him some time, but he eventually won back over the Kings who had joined with the Silvers—all except the King of Silvers."

"And his name was?" she asked.

"Ulrik." Cináed let himself think about that day for a brief moment. The smoke, the blood and death, and the screams of both humans and dragons would never leave him. It was a memory that was embedded in his mind, one that would forever replay no matter how many millennia passed.

"What happened?"

Cináed realized he had stopped talking and let the memories take him. He cleared his throat and put a hand behind his head. "There was no way the dragons and humans could co-exist anymore. Con knew it. So he called the Kings together and had them use their magic to build a dragon bridge to another realm. Then they sent the dragons across it."

"Even the Silvers? Wouldn't they stay with their King?"

"Aye. They did. But Constantine is King of Dragon Kings, so he could overrule even their King. All but four of the largest Silvers obeyed and went over the bridge. That left the Kings only Ulrik and the remaining four Silvers to deal with. The Kings made the Silvers sleep and trapped them in a mountain."

She lowered her legs to the bed again. "And Ulrik?"

"Con stripped him of his magic so that he would remain only in human form. Then he banished Ulrik from the Kings' domain. Ulrik had no choice but to live among the mortals, becoming one of them. For millions of years, that's exactly what happened. And through all this, the magic of this realm found its way to a select few humans who learned how to use it. They became Druids. When the war broke out with the dragons, many of the Druids fled to Skye."

"I see," Gemma said with a smile. "And the Fae fit in how?"

"After the dragons left, the Kings disappeared, hiding away from the mortals until any memory of them passed into legend and myth. When they eventually emerged, they had to find their way in the world once more."

Gemma lifted a shoulder. "Except this time without their dragons."

Cináed nodded, glad she said the words so he didn't have to. "Con kept to their vow of protection despite everything. It was a good thing too, because when the Fae arrived they went straight for the humans."

"I don't understand," she said.

"The Fae are divided into two sects. Light and Dark. The Light have silver eyes and black hair. The Dark have red eyes and silver streaks in their black hair. The more silver, the more evil they've done. But both sects are stunningly beautiful. Mortals are drawn to both Dark and Light Fae. The Light make sure that they only have sex with mortals once, but even that is enough to ruin a human from ever feeling any pleasure with another of their kind again."

Gemma made a face. "And the Dark?"

"They feed off humans by having sex. The more they have sex with a mortal, the more they drain the person of their soul until nothing is left but a husk."

She gave a little shiver. "You would think that if this happens that humans would blast it all over the place to warn others."

"But they doona. Luckily, the Dragon Kings stepped in. They went to war with the Dark, and after many months, the Light joined the Kings and defeated the Dark, pushing them to Ireland."

She snorted. "Ireland? Why didn't the Kings send them away?"

"There was a truce. The Fae agreed to remain in Ireland, and the Kings got the humans out. Except mortals returned there despite the Kings' attempts."

"So the Fae and Druids have free rein of this world."

Cináed shrugged one shoulder. "In a way."

"And the Kings?"

"Remain hidden."

Her gaze moved away as she nodded. "Why?"

"It's what they've chosen."

"Maybe that's not the right path."

"There can be no co-existence of dragons and humans."

Gemma issued a bark of laughter. "Seems like Druids, Fae, humans, and Kings have been co-existing for some time."

He'd never thought of it that way. "I'm no' sure I'd call it co-existing."

"Humans live together and fight constantly. That's what all of us are doing, no matter what species we are. But I'm curious. Why did the Fae come here?"

"Civil war between the Light and Dark destroyed their world. I suspect they followed the humans here, but that's just my speculation."

She blew out a breath and lightly caressed his chest. "I think you might be right. Where does this leave me? You say I'm a Clacher, but I have no magic."

"I'm no' sure. I'm hoping the Druids here on Skye might be able to help."

Gemma nodded her head. "We'll see. Do you have any idea on what happened to my family?"

"I think it was a Druid or a Fae. It was a Druid who wiped out the Clacher line, but that Druid is long dead."

"Someone else could have taken up the mantle," Gemma said.

Cináed twisted his lips. "That's certainly a possibility. Corann, the leader of the Skye Druids, is pretty knowledgeable about the goings-on. If he can no' help us, then we'll have to go another route."

"Sounds good. So, when are you going to tell me that you're a Dragon King?"

He blinked, taken aback by her words. "What?"

"It's obvious," she said. "The way you spoke about the Kings, your knowledge of them. That wasn't a story passed down. You lived it. And then there's your tattoo."

Cináed stared into her blue eyes.

"You should have told me. I would still have listened to the story. Then you could have told it from your perspective."

"I did," he murmured.

She leaned forward and put her hand on his cheek. "You kept your feelings out of it. But it was there in your eyes and the set of your jaw. I felt your pain when you described the dragons going over the bridge to another realm. I'm sorry you had to go through that."

He shrugged, unsure of what to say. "It's done."

"You will always carry it. Just as I've carried all of what happened to me so long ago. Maybe that's why I feel such a pull toward you. You understand me."

"Or it could be something else entirely," he said as he tugged her down for a kiss.

She lay out alongside him and moaned. "Or it could be something else entirely," she repeated.

Chapter Eighteen

Magic. The word swirled through Gemma's mind while she slept securely in Cináed's arms. It was also the first thing on her mind when she woke the next morning.

She wasn't surprised to find that Cináed was already awake. He rolled her onto her back and gazed down at her. The fanciful part of her wanted to call the look wonder, but she might be reading too much into it.

"Damn, you're beautiful," he murmured and smoothed her hair back from her face.

Her heart swelled. Being with him was everything. He made her feel special and cared for—and it had nothing to do with him being a Dragon King and everything to do with the person he was.

"I'd like nothing more than to stay right here in this bed and make love to you all day," he said.

Gemma ran her fingers along the scruff on his cheek. "Me, too. I'd give almost anything if the outside world wouldn't intrude."

"If that's what you really want I can make it happen."

The fact that he not only offered but actually could give her that made her fall for him even more. "Maybe after we sort through my history we could return?"

"Absolutely," he replied with a grin.

"I guess that means I need to get up."

"That would probably be wise since Corann is here."

Her heart missed a beat. "The Druid leader? He's here? How?"

"He's a Druid."

As if that explained everything. Then again, maybe it did. Gemma had a lot to learn about Druids. She sat up as Cináed moved off the bed to stand. "How did he know we were here?"

"That was probably Merrill."

"Merrill is here?"

"He's been with us the entire time."

She scooted to the end of the bed and grabbed for the bag of clothes she had brought. "I might have been preoccupied and distracted, but I would know if there had been another person with us."

Cináed tugged the shirt over his head and pulled it down before fastening the dark denim. "He's been in the water. This entire area was his domain."

"Water?" She gave a shake of her head. "Dragons live in water?"

"Dragons live everywhere. Some of us prefer mountains, some deserts, some forests, some water, and everything in between."

She swallowed and began to dress. "So when you said you and Merrill went diving, you didn't mean with scuba tanks."

"Nay. We're able to go down to depths no mortal ever could on their own."

"I see." She inwardly gave a shake of her head as she quickly finished getting ready. After brushing out her hair she pulled it into a ponytail.

Then she faced him. "I'm ready."

He walked to her and pulled her into his arms for a slow kiss. "I doona know what we're going to learn, if anything."

"I can handle it," she assured him. And she hoped she could.

He gave her a nod and took her hand as they walked to the door. Cináed opened it, and waited for her to step through. As soon as she did she spotted a man with his back to her. He had stark white hair, and was a little bent with age. The man turned and faced them, showing his long white beard and the staff he held in one hand.

"It's Gandalf," she said before she could think better of it.

Cináed laughed, and the man joined in.

"Ah, my child, many have called me that," he said as he walked toward them. "I doona mind at all." He stopped before her and looked her over with his eyes full of knowledge and secrets. "You must be Gemma."

She glanced at Cináed and nodded. "I am. I've never met a Druid before. I'm not sure what I expected, but it wasn't this."

Corann threw back his head and laughed. "I like your honesty. We're going to get on well."

"Come inside so we can talk," Cináed said.

"Yes, yes," Corann said. "More weather is coming our way."

Gemma looked to the sky but saw only blue with the occasional white cloud. But who was she to argue with a Druid? She fell in step behind Corann. The entire time Cináed kept a hold of her hand. She liked that.

Once inside, Cináed directed her toward the table where Corann already sat. She pulled out one of the chairs and swallowed nervously. When she realized Cináed was making tea she wished she was the one doing it so she wouldn't be sitting there so awkwardly.

"We've met, you know."

Her gaze jerked to the Druid. "We have?"

"You were just a wee thing. I helped your parents buy the isle believing, as your father did, that you all would be safe there."

Gemma wanted to believe him, but she wasn't sure if she could. It didn't make sense really. She wanted answers, and Corann was giving them to her. Yet, it almost seemed too easy.

Cináed set cups down on the table and filled each of them with tea before he sat next to her. The entire time, no one spoke.

It was Corann who broke the silence. "I didna contact you all these years because I knew you wouldna believe anything I had to say, Gemma. Your father spent his life hiding, as did every member of his family before him. He expected to continue like that, and he intended to let the line die out with him. Then he met your mother. Their love was undeniable, and with that realization, he knew he had to reevaluate his life."

Gemma's hand suddenly grew cold. She wrapped her hand around the cup, letting the warmth seep into her. "You helped my family?"

"I did," Corann said with a nod of his white head.

Cináed grinned as he nodded. "You're the Ben Sinclair I found through the documentations."

Corann smiled. "The verra one."

"If you were such a good friend, then where were you that night they disappeared?" Gemma demanded.

Corann's eyes lowered to the table as he let out a sigh. Finally, he lifted his gaze to her. "I wish I had a proper answer, but I doona. You can plan every detail, but there will always be something that doesna go as you expect or hope. The night your family disappeared, we were attacked here."

Cináed's brows furrowed deeply. "You were? By who?"

"I doona know."

Gemma snorted at that, looking between the two men. "You can't be serious. You're a Druid, and you don't know who attacked you?"

"No." Corann sat back in his chair and made a face. "No amount of our magic was able to decipher who the culprits were."

"They used magic to hide themselves," Cináed guessed.

Corann nodded his head of white hair. "They did. For a moment, I thought it was the Kings."

Cináed gave him a flat look. "We wouldna do such a thing."

"I realized that soon enough."

Gemma asked, "That leaves who, then? Fae or other Druids?"

"Aye," Cináed said.

She leaned forward to pour milk into her tea. "What does each have to gain from attacking here?"

"It wasna just here," Cináed said. "It was your isle as well."

Corann drank his tea and set the cup on the table. "No matter how I've looked at the attack, I always came back to your family, Gemma. Whoever did this knew I was helping you, which seems unlikely since I kept that confidential from everyone. But there is no other connection."

"They wanted to keep you away from helping Gemma and her family," Cináed said.

"That's right," the elder Druid mumbled.

She felt the eyes of both men on her. "If you're hoping I have some answers, I don't. I was a child."

Cináed's hand covered hers. "We doona think that. Tell Corann what you saw that night."

"You saw them?" the Druid asked as he sat forward, eager to hear more.

She winced. "Not really. And there was just one."

Corann's white brows drew together as his forehead furrowed. "Only one?"

Gemma didn't miss the exchange between him and Cináed. "At first, I didn't see anything. It was just something I felt. It made even my dog shake."

"Evil," Corann said.

"This was at the dock where my parents and Kyle had been, but there was nothing there. The storm continued to get worse and the waves were growing higher. I wanted to go out on the dock to see if I could see the boat, but there was something there. So I ran. It was the lightning that showed me the silhouette. I couldn't tell if it was a man or a woman. When I fell in the water, it came to the edge, waiting for me. I knew it was there to kill me, so I held my breath as long as I could before I surfaced. It must have believed I died, because it wasn't there."

The Druid shook his head, squeezing his eyes closed briefly. "Oh, dear child. I'm so sorry I wasna there to help."

"My family is dead, aren't they?" Gemma needed to know. It felt as if everyone had tiptoed around the issue. It was time to ask the difficult question.

Cináed squeezed her hand. "I believe so, aye."

She had long suspected that, but hearing the words caused emotion to choke her. When Cináed pulled her toward him so he could wrap his arms around her, she didn't stop him. They remained like that for a long time while the three sat in silence.

Gemma finally lifted her gaze to meet the sad eyes of Corann. "Are there Druids powerful enough to have accomplished what happened here on Skye and my isle?"

"There are two I can think of," Corann said. "One is mated to a Dragon King, but at that time, she would have been only a child herself."

"And the other?" Gemma asked.

Cináed said, "Isla."

Corann gave a single nod. "She wasna involved."

Gemma hated being excluded. "Who is Isla?"

"She's married to a Warrior," Cináed said.

"A what?"

Cináed's face creased in regret. "I might have forgotten to mention them. They also have magic from the primeval gods inside them."

"What Cináed is trying to say is that Isla was with Hayden at MacLeod Castle. I went to Isla and asked her if she had anything to do with the attack after it happened. She didna, nor did any Druid at MacLeod Castle."

Cináed blew out a breath. "Is there any other Druid with such abilities that you doona know about?"

"There is always that chance. I'm no' all seeing."

Gemma's head was beginning to ache. "If it wasn't a Druid, then it has to be Fae."

"It can no' be," Corann said harshly.

He then rose to his feet and walked to the window to gaze out of it. Gemma slid her eyes to Cináed, hoping he might shed some light on what had just happened.

"Corann and his Druids guard the Fairy Pool here on Skye. The pool is the gateway to the Fae. They've had a connection for as long as there have been Druids here and Fae on this realm," Cináed explained.

Now she understood. "If it was a Fae, then that means they betrayed you, Corann."

"Yes," he murmured. He turned to face her. "I've no' wanted to believe that possible, but it looks as if it might verra well be."

"Why though?" Gemma asked.

A muscle in Cináed's jaw clenched. "The Others."

Corann's eyes narrowed. "Why would they worry about the Clachers?"

"That's a verra good question," Cináed said.

Gemma shook her head in frustration. "What are the Others?"

"A group of Light and Dark Fae and *mie* and *drough* Druids who have taken up a quest to destroy the Dragon Kings," Corann explained.

Gemma met Cináed's gaze. "Why would they care about my family? We had no connection to the Kings."

"That we know of," Cináed said.

Chapter Nineteen

They were missing something. Cináed was sure of it. If only he could figure out what it was. Corann had done wonders in filling in some of the blanks, but it wasn't enough.

"Take me back to the isle," Gemma said.

Cináed was shocked at her statement. "Why?"

"I want this ended. I want to know it's over."

Corann put an arm on the table and cocked his head. "What are you thinking?"

"I'm thinking that if I go there and let it be known that I'm back, whoever came for my parents will return."

Cináed was having none of that. "And then they'll come for you. That's no' a good idea."

"It's because you and Merrill will be there," she said.

He wished he had some argument to dissuade her, but she had a point. If he and Merrill were hiding in the water, they just might get whoever had come after her family. It was a big maybe, however.

Corann then asked, "And what if no one comes?"

Gemma shrugged her shoulders. "Then no one comes. But as you said, everyone in my family has always hidden, and they came after my parents and brother. I got away. Don't you think they'd want to finish the job?"

"She's got a point," the Druid told Cináed.

Cináed knew it, but he wasn't so sure he wanted to give voice to his thoughts. By Gemma's own admission, she had barely gotten away the first time the entity came for her. Fate had favored her that day, but would it again?

Especially now that the Kings knew Usaeil, Queen of the Light, was part of the Others? If she got wind of Gemma...or worse, if she was the one who had gone after Gemma's family, then there would be little that prevented Usaeil from getting to Gemma this time.

Was luck on their side this time? They had reached the isle unseen—or so he hoped. More troubling was why this entity had allowed Gemma to live.

"I think we're playing with fire," Cináed cautioned.

Corann's eyes narrowed on him. "What are you no' telling me? I know all about the Others from Rhi."

"There is something we've intentionally no' told you."

"Then I think you might want to rectify that."

Cináed shook his head, feeling Gemma's eyes on him. "I can no'. It's for your own safety."

The Druid slowly sat back. "You know some of the Fae involved with the Others."

It wasn't a question. Cináed nodded, letting the leader of the Druids know at least that much.

"I understand," he said.

"Hold on," Gemma said as she looked from one to the other, her pale blue orbs landing on him last. "Did you just nix my plan?"

Cináed drew in a breath and tried to find the right words. "It willna be safe."

"I want to know who came after me that night. I want to know if they did indeed kill my family. I think I have that right."

"You doona understand the full power of the Others."

She raised a brow. "Are you afraid of them?"

"Nay," he stated more angrily than he wanted. "I know what they can do. Their combined magic is greater than that of a Dragon King's."

"And that's never been done before," Corann added.

Some of the wind went out of Gemma's sails at that point. "Still, you're guessing this is a Fae, and you're guessing that it's the Others. Don't you want to know who it is and why? Don't you want to see if it is the Others and what connection my family has to the Kings?"

Damn her for pointing that out. Cináed wanted to tell her no, that none of it mattered. But the Kings needed all the information they could get on the Others. So far everything they had was bits and pieces they picked up along the way.

Corann caught his gaze. "I can be there, and if need be, I can bring some Druids."

"That would only complicate things," Cináed said.

Gemma shook her head in obvious confusion. "How? Wouldn't the more people that were there to fight be better?"

"If who I think will be there shows up, then Corann and the Skye Druids will be next on the list to be wiped out. Magic is fading on this realm. We need the Druids."

Her head swiveled to the Druid as she raised a brow.

Corann nodded slowly. "Cináed's right. Magic is fading. Druid bloodlines are mixing with those without magic, diluting it until there are fewer and fewer born with magic. Some of those that have enough to be aware of it doona even know they're Druids, so they can no' be trained."

"You mean like how I don't have magic," she said.

Corann gave her a comforting smile. "My dear, the Clachers had a unique ability that, in many ways, outshone and out-powered that of any Druid. They could detect Druids. They were able to find the truth in something and make sure that justice was served."

"I'm sorry that my family failed in that regard. Is that why the Clachers were wiped out? Because they knew no one would be able to take their place?" she asked Cináed.

"Until you, we believed that there were no other Clachers in that bloodline. We have a brother and sister, Henry and Esther, at Dreagan who have taken up the mantle of the Clachers. We've been trying to see if we can trace their family line back to the Clachers, but it's been difficult."

The news didn't seem to sit well with Gemma. "Oh. I see."

"That doesna mean you are no' important," Cináed said. "You could be the last descendent of that line."

She shrugged. "Or not. Henry and Esther might be. They are, after all, doing what my ancestors did."

Cináed watched as she rose and walked from the house. His eyes followed her, wondering what he had said that had gone so wrong. When he looked to the old Druid, Corann rolled his eyes.

"For just a moment, she felt as if she were part of something," Corann explained. "Even without her brother, she meant something."

Cináed pffted at that. "She means something now. With her blood, she could carry on the Clacher dynasty."

"And what of Henry and Esther?"

Cináed hadn't thought of that. Now he understood why Gemma was upset. He looked out the window at her standing with her back to him and her arms crossed. The wind lifted the locks of her ponytail, sending her ginger hair waving.

"I know that look. You're going to take her to the isle and make it known that Gemma is there," Corann said.

Cináed ran a hand down his face. "I am. She deserves answers after so long with nothing."

"I will do my best to help however I can."

"Keep your Druids and yourself safe."

Corann grabbed for the staff that he'd leaned near the door when he entered. "You keep her safe."

"Doona worry. I will."

Cináed stood as Corann walked from the house. He held back while the Druid went to Gemma and spoke a few words to her. Then he began to make his way over the land.

After a few minutes, Cináed moved to stand beside Gemma. "I doona want you in any kind of danger. I believe you experienced enough that one night, but I understand your need for answers. And while you doona believe you're essential in this world, you would be wrong." He turned his head to find her looking at him. "A Druid went to great lengths to wipe your ancestors from existence. Someone else recently tried to do the same. Your line has survived. Whether it was luck, Fate, or the hand of some powerful being, you're standing here."

"When you say it like that, it's a little daunting. I feel like the entire world is looking at me," she said.

He shifted to face her. "You have shouldered so verra much on your own and stood tall while doing it. Doona let this sway you now."

"I can't help it," she said with a shrug. Then she faced him, dropping her arms to her sides. "Am I insane wanting to call out this person?"

"You want answers."

"That's not what I asked."

He blew out a breath and glanced to the side. "I'm no' sure I'm the right person to ask. I doona want you in any sort of danger, but if I were in your position, I'd go."

"All this time I've known my family was dead, but I'd held out hope. Even the thought of them leaving me behind was better than knowing they were gone forever."

"You have a responsibility to carry on the line."

She blinked up at him. "Why? My father was prepared to let the line die with him. Maybe that would be the best thing. Why make anyone else live in seclusion, always hiding and looking over their shoulder?"

"It's no' a good life, that's for sure. But the Clachers were important. *You're* important," he added.

"Not so much," she replied with a smile. "With Henry and Esther taking the duties my family once had, I mean nothing."

He closed the small distance between them. "Gemma, there is power in your blood. The proof lay in the fact that someone once tried to erase you from the world."

"Maybe. I don't care about that."

She might not, but he certainly did. He saw the big picture. And perhaps, if he could connect the dots to the Clachers and Dragon Kings, he might help her see it as well.

He reached for her, pulling her against him. His eyes closed when her arms went around him and her cheek lay against his chest. This was where she belonged. In his arms.

Cináed held her tighter. He'd known she was special the moment he saw that photo of her as a child. But getting to know her had shown him she was more than he'd ever expected. The very thing he hadn't even been thinking of finding—his mate.

She was the one he would love until the end of time. He wanted to tell her, to share how he felt, but he hesitated. She had just opened up to him. To push her now might mean he lost her forever.

"I'll no' let any harm come to you," he vowed.

Her hands rubbed up and down his back. "I know. It's the only reason I have the courage to go to the isle again." She lifted her head to look at him. "When it's all finished, can we return here?"

"We can go anywhere you want."

"I just want to be with you."

"Sounds perfect," he said with a grin.

She returned his smile, but it soon died. "I don't want to wait. Let's get it over with."

He gave a nod and made his way to the chopper as she went back inside to get her bag. Cináed used that time to contact Merrill through their link.

"*It's about time,*" Merrill stated irritably. "*What's going on?*"

"*A lot has happened.*"

"*Then you best tell me.*"

Cináed quickly recounted what had occurred since he and Gemma left the isle yesterday.

"*Bloody hell. You're really going to let her do this?*" Merrill asked.

"*It's no' my life.*"

"*That's a load of shite. You know you could stop her. Easily.*"

"*Aye,*" Cináed agreed. "*I could. But to what end? She would make her way back here eventually. At least we'll be here. Then there's the added benefit of finding out who attacked her and the Skye Druids.*"

Merrill snorted loudly. "*My bet is on the Light bitch. She's addled in the head, brother.*"

"*Without a doubt. But knowledge is power.*"

"*I'm on my way to the isle. I didna find any spells when I looked yesterday, but I'll do another sweep anyway.*"

Cináed smiled. "*Thanks. I'll join you shortly.*"

"*You might want to rethink that and stay with her.*"

He had a point. Cináed grunted. "*I'll consider it.*"

The link severed as Gemma climbed into the helicopter and buckled herself in. Cináed started the engines. In no time they were in the air and headed back to the isle.

Unease ran through him. Things could go so very wrong. But there was also a chance that they could learn something important regarding the Others.

Discovering all the Fae involved was imperative, because if they had those identities, it was just a matter of eliminating them. Whatever Druids were still involved wouldn't matter without the Fae to bind them together.

Cináed looked over at Gemma. She stared straight ahead, determination in her eyes and the way she held her head. If anyone could do this, it was her.

And he was going to make sure she succeeded.

Chapter Twenty

The wind seemed colder. Gemma knew it was only in her mind. Or was it? Was it just her imagination that the air around her isle was chillier, as if something sinister had never left the area?

She stood inside the house, waiting. But she didn't know what for. Corann had said a storm was coming. When she had looked, the sky had been clear, but now it was filled with ominous dark clouds.

A shiver raced down her spine, causing her to wrap her arms around herself. Maybe it was because she stood alone to alert the entity that she was there, but she wished she hadn't told Cináed to hide now. She would be handling things better if she weren't by herself.

That caused her to snort loudly. All these years she had declared to herself and anyone who asked that she didn't need anyone, that she was perfectly capable of dealing with anything on her own.

But being with Cináed showed her the truth.

While she *could* do things herself, it was better when she had someone she could trust beside her.

Trust. She shook her head, smiling. He'd told her he would gain her trust. And he had. Entirely too easily. Then again, she hadn't stood a chance because it felt as if she had always known him.

The distant rumble of thunder had her heart quickening. Everything inside her was screaming to run away, to leave and never return. But she had been running for too long. She claimed it was because she liked to move around, but that was a lie.

Fear had ruled her life. She'd gotten too used to the emotion that not only had it become a part of her world, but she needed reminding that it was there.

No longer would she hide away from the world. No longer would she shy away from the memories when they came. She was a new person.

Now she was facing the past and all the secrets it held.

Now she would confront the monster who had destroyed her life.

Now she would become the warrior her ancestors had been—and died as.

Gemma dropped her arms to her sides and walked out of the house she had loved so dearly. She looked up at the sky, her gaze moving from cloud to cloud. "I know you can hear me. You killed my parents and my brother, but you missed me. I'm back to claim my heritage as a Clacher. And I'm ready for you. Bring your worst."

In response, a gust of wind angrily blew against her. She didn't move. Her eyes lowered to the water. Cináed and Merrill were there, waiting and watching to keep her safe. She hadn't asked if they were in their true forms or not. Now she wished she had.

Just as she wished she had asked Cináed what color his dragon was.

Gemma still couldn't believe he was a Dragon King. She wanted to see him, the real Cináed. Not that his human form wasn't mouthwateringly gorgeous. But to see *him*...yeah, that was going to be amazing.

She was so lost in thoughts of Cináed that the pelting of rain on her face came as a shock. Her gaze lifted to see one of the large black clouds settled right over her.

"There was a storm yesterday," she told herself. "This means nothing."

Although she had just challenged the being who'd killed her family. She knew next to nothing about magic, but something had told her to verbalize her defiance.

The water around the isle grew choppier. The waves white-capped as they hurtled toward land, slamming into the rocks and onto the beach. It was so similar to the night her family vanished that she nearly let the fear choke her.

But Gemma stood strong. She lifted her chin as she thought about the ancient line she came from. A line of honorable, respected people.

"I'm a Clacher," she told herself, grasping for any amount of courage she could find. "I come from an ancient line who kept order within the Druids. Twice we have been targeted for eradication. And twice we've survived. The strength of my ancestors runs through my veins. And they stand beside me."

The tips of her fingers began to tingle. And even more oddly, she could have sworn that she wasn't alone, that her forebears were, indeed, with her.

While the wind whipped the water that went from a drizzle to rain in all directions, Gemma stood firm. She wasn't going to run inside and cower. If it was her day to die, then she would do it with dignity.

But if it was her day to fight, then she was going to give whatever came for her hell.

Out of nowhere, a man appeared to her left. His short silver hair had barely any black left in it. But it was the flashing red eyes that let her know she was facing a Dark Fae.

He was a handsome specimen, but he was nothing compared to Cináed. So when the Dark smiled at her, she just stared at him. His head cocked to the side, his eyes narrowing as he took a step closer.

"Trying to fight the attraction, sweetheart? It won't work."

She frowned at the sound of his Irish accent. It sounded rough and rudimentary to her ears. Gemma didn't bother to respond. He didn't look like someone who would pay attention to what she said anyway.

"Go ahead and take off your clothes," he ordered.

Her brow quirked. "I'll pass."

That stopped him in his tracks. He looked her up and down. "You don't want me?"

"I can see that has shocked you."

Red eyes slowly moved around the area. "You're not Fae. That means you...." His gaze snapped to her face. "You've been with a Dragon King."

She smiled and shrugged. "Guilty."

"Where is he?"

Gemma spread her arms wide. "Not here."

"No way he'd leave you to me."

She kept waiting for that evil feeling to assault her again, but she felt nothing but disgust at this individual. There was no doubt he was wicked, but it wasn't the same maliciousness that she'd felt that night.

He sneered at her. "You have to die. I was going to have some fun with it, but you've ruined that."

"So sorry to disappoint. You'll forgive me if I don't care about your plans. I have some of my own."

"You?" he said with a laugh. "What can a measly human do to me?"

Gemma cocked her head at him. "Was it you all those years ago?

Were you the one who did it?"

"Did what?" he asked angrily. "This is the first time I've been on this isle."

Just as she thought. "Then go back to whoever sent you and tell them to come themselves. I'll be waiting."

"It doesn't work that way, sweetheart." He smiled then. "Trust me. You'd rather me kill you."

"Yeah, I don't think so. I came here to confront the one who murdered my family."

The Dark threw back his head and laughed. "You're entertaining if nothing else."

Gemma lifted her chin. She knew nothing about fighting. In fact, she hadn't thought about what she was going to do to whoever showed up. Obviously, she should've thought this through better.

"You don't scare me. I'm a Clacher," she stated.

The Dark held out his hand as an iridescent orb appeared. At her words, he stilled, a deep frown forming. "What did you say?"

"I'm Gemma Clacher." The fact the Fae hesitated made her take a step toward him. "What does that name mean to you?"

From the corner of her eye, she saw something walking toward her out of the rain. She glanced toward the figure to see it was Cináed. The Dark was too focused on her to realize they were no longer alone.

"I'd like to know the answer myself," Cináed said when he reached them.

The Dark's head jerked toward Cináed. "I knew you wouldn't leave the female after you'd claimed her."

"Answer her," Cináed demanded.

The Fae laughed as he looked between them. "I don't think so."

Gemma opened her mouth, but before she got any words out, Cináed had the Dark on his back. The orb rolled from the Fae's hands, singeing the ground and turning it black while wisps of smoke rose from it with every drop of rain.

Cináed's hand was around the Dark's throat squeezing. And the look of retribution that flashed in Cináed's eyes made her heart skip a beat.

She'd seen the tender side of him, the sweet side, and even the determined side. This was another aspect that she hadn't witnessed before. But she liked it.

A lot.

This strength and power was why Cináed was a Dragon King. He didn't show it all the time, but it was always there, ready and waiting to take on any threat.

Gemma took a few quick steps back when Cináed and the Dark began to fight. They rolled on the ground, each getting in hits, and both coming dangerously close to the orb. But all that changed in an instant when the Fae produced another bubble and slammed it into Cináed's chest.

She gasped when Cináed's shirt and skin began to hiss as if burned. He bared his teeth, his jaw clenching before he knocked the Fae's hand away. And that's when she saw the burn. It went all the way through his muscle to bone. The pain must be unbearable, and yet Cináed didn't pause for a moment.

He merely grasped the Dark's head and twisted. The crack of bone was loud, even over the rain.

Gemma stared at the Dark, waiting to see if he would rise. Cináed climbed to his feet and started toward her. He got two steps before he stopped and swiveled his head to the side.

"Get ready," he warned her.

She blinked through the rain, trying to see what he saw. "For what?"

He didn't answer. Instead, he held his hand over the orb that remained. It lifted in the air, coming towards his palm. Just before it touched him, he reared his hand back and sent it flying.

The strangled cry of pain reached them a second later. In the next heartbeat, two more Dark appeared.

Cináed motioned her behind him. She did as he requested, even as she glanced at his wound. If that's what the bubble could do to him, she needed to make certain one never touched her.

Her mind stopped when the Fae reached Cináed and the three were engaged in hand-to-hand combat. But it was more than punches and elbows. There was magic involved, making things even more difficult.

She felt insignificant and in the way. There was nothing she could do to help, which made things even worse for her. Not that Cináed wasn't handling it brilliantly all by himself. Besides, if he needed help, Merrill was there to lend a hand.

Or was it claw?

She inwardly gave herself a shake. Now was not the time.

Her mind went blank when she felt it behind her. The cloying, sickening coils of evil reaching for her. Gemma shouted Cináed's name over and over in her head, but nothing went past her lips.

Slowly, she turned and looked over her shoulder. At first she saw nothing but sheets of rain. Then, a form took shape. That of a beautiful woman. Long black hair fell around her without a single drop of rain reaching her. Gemma found herself staring into silver eyes that changed to red.

"We finally meet, Gemma," she said.

The smile the Fae bestowed upon her made Gemma want to vomit. She wanted to run, to flee, but her feet were rooted to the ground. Her mind went back to that night when her family died. This...Fae...was responsible. Gemma knew it to the bottom of her soul.

Somehow, she swallowed the fear. She fisted her hands to keep them from shaking. Then, she took a step forward. It was a small one, but it was a step. "I escaped you once."

"Did you?" the Fae asked, brow raised. Her laugh sent ice through Gemma's veins. "I admit, I did believe you drowned. But I saw the papers. I knew you lived."

"Why didn't you come for me?"

The woman's eyes moved past her to Cináed. Gemma's stomach fell to her feet. "No."

"Oh, yes," the Fae said.

Chapter Twenty-one

"Cináed!"

The panic and distress he heard in Gemma's voice went through him like a blade. He finished off the final Dark and whirled around.

Only to see Usaeil standing behind Gemma.

He'd known the Queen of the Light was involved, and now he had proof. He immediately sent out a message through the link to all Dragon Kings.

His gaze met Gemma's. When she mouthed for him to leave, he knew that it had all been a trap. No doubt Usaeil intended to kill Gemma, but Cináed couldn't imagine what she thought she would do to him.

"Cináed? What's going on?" Merrill asked.

"It's a trap by Usaeil. Stay hidden for now. You may be the only thing that saves Gemma."

"What about you?"

"It's time someone finds out what the Light bitch wants."

There was a pause. *"Tell her we know she's with the Others."*

"I don't want to give that information away quite yet."

"Good point. Be careful, brother."

The link severed. Cináed fisted his hands against the wounds all over his body inflicted by the Darks' magic. They would heal, but not as quickly as he would like. Especially when he faced off against Usaeil.

"You honestly believed I didn't know she was alive?" Usaeil asked him with a smug grin.

Cináed wished Gemma was beside him. As it was, she was closer to the queen than him, and that didn't sit well at all. "You allowed her to live."

"I intended to kill her that night with the rest of her family."

He glanced at Gemma to see tears rolling down her face. But it wasn't sadness, it was anger that contorted her features. She kept her back to Usaeil and her eyes locked on him. He didn't dare take a step to her. Nor could he beckon Gemma to him with Usaeil watching.

Cináed decided to give Gemma some closure about that night. "Why come after them? They were hidden, the Clacher gift gone."

"You don't know." Usaeil's smile grew with that knowledge. "Imagine that. The mighty Dragon Kings missing a vital piece of the puzzle."

He filed that bit of information away. It had been apparent the Clachers were significant, and while he didn't know how—yet—the fact that he discovered that they were meant the Kings were one step closer to uncovering another clue.

Cináed grinned. "We might no' have known that, but it doesna take much to get you to talk about things. Your vanity takes little prodding to get you to admit such valuable information."

"Careful," Usaeil said, her smile gone. "Your ego might overshadow you."

"It would have to be big indeed for that to happen," he taunted.

Usaeil's red eyes narrowed. "You hate me now, but soon that will change. Soon you'll see what I can give the Dragon Kings."

"Give us?" he asked with a laugh.

"You won't be laughing for long, Cináed."

That gave him pause. Rain dripped from his lashes. He blinked them away.

"I knew by allowing Gemma to live that one day everything would fall into place. I didn't know how or why, but I knew being patient would grant me something big simply because of her bloodline. I never expected it to be the Kings. All it took was nudging her toward Dreagan."

It was much more than that, but Cináed didn't bother to try and explain. Usaeil wouldn't understand that if he had never been looking for information on the Others that he wouldn't have seen Gemma's picture, and therefore would never have gone looking for her.

Unable to help himself, he moved his gaze to Gemma. He wanted her to know that he was proud of her courage. It took more than most would ever pull together to do what she had done—was still doing.

If only he could give her a nod or something, but he didn't want to give Usaeil any ammunition to use against him. Because she would. In a heartbeat.

Suddenly, Gemma smiled at him. As if she knew he'd been thinking about her. He couldn't return the grin, no matter how much he wanted to.

Usaeil rolled her eyes. "Shouldn't you be asking me questions, Cináed? Perhaps what I think I can do for the Kings?"

"There's no need. You want me to know badly enough that you'll tell me regardless." He moved his gaze to her.

Her beauty was without a doubt, but her soul was as black as they came. How had Con missed that when he'd given in and taken her to his bed? Then again, there were many things Con did that Cináed didn't agree with—until he learned everything.

The thing about Con was that he kept so much to himself. Cináed suspected that it was more than Con being lonely that turned the King of Dragon Kings to the Queen of the Light. And he couldn't wait to find out what that was.

Anger rolled off the queen in waves. She wasn't at all amused by Cináed's comment, despite it being the truth.

Usaeil cocked a hip and put a hand on it. "This show all you Kings continue to do in front of me is for naught. Con knows he's mine."

"Did he ever say it?" Cináed asked.

"He didn't have to. It was in his actions every time he came to my bed."

Gemma laughed, causing Cináed to inwardly wince. Usaeil's gaze slid to Gemma, her eyes narrowing. Just as the queen was remembering why she was on the isle, he turned her attention back to him.

"Sex isna love," Cináed stated. "Just because Con used your body for some relief doesna mean he wants you as his mate."

Just as he expected, the jab shifted Usaeil's interest back to him. He kept his gaze on the queen, but his attention never left Gemma. That was the only reason he saw her slowly inching her way toward him.

"I will be his mate." Thunder rumbled after Usaeil's declaration. "I am meant to be his. The Fae and dragons will unite. Those unions will not only give each of you the children you've never had, but it will keep the magic flowing on this realm."

"You're a complete nutter."

Usaeil scoffed at his words. "We'll see who's insane when everything I say comes to pass."

"You're forgetting one thing. Con has to want you for his mate. And he doesna."

"That's where you're wrong."

Cináed realized that nothing he said was going to make a difference. So he decided to play along with her. "Say the Light and Kings do unite. What then?"

"Meaning?"

He waved his hand, indicating her red eyes that indicated to one and all that she was Dark, not Light. "This."

She laughed softly. "That will be taken care of shortly."

"Meaning?"

A black brow quirked. "You don't actually think I'm going to tell you all of my plans, do you?"

"As a matter of fact, I do."

"You'd be wrong. What I will tell you is that I'll be taking what I allowed to live all these years—Gemma. The Clacher line ends today."

Cináed dove towards Gemma, wrapping his arms around her and twisting as they fell to take the brunt of the fall. He grunted when Usaeil's magic landed on his side.

"Stay near me," he said to Gemma before he jumped to his feet.

"Stand in my way and you will fail," Usaeil told him.

Cináed took a deep breath. "We'll see about that."

* * * *

If the fight earlier with the Dark had been eye-opening, it was nothing compared to this. The air crackled with hostile tensions.

Gemma took a step back to give Cináed room as he widened his stance. The most nerve-wracking thing she'd ever done was standing still while listening to the exchange between him and the queen, who, she had to agree, was indeed off her rocker.

Gemma glanced at Cináed's back to see his shirt falling off and his body blackened with several wounds—one of which was on his side and looked newer than the others.

"Give me the mortal," Usaeil said to Cináed. "And I'll let you go back to Dreagan."

Cináed snorted. "You can no' stop me."

"You want to take a chance on that?"

"I do."

Gemma took another step back. She looked over her shoulder to make sure no one was there even though it felt as if someone watched them. She didn't get the feeling that whoever it was wanted to harm her. In fact, she had the distinct impression they were there for Usaeil.

She returned her attention to Cináed in time to see him twist to avoid being hit with another of those orbs, which she figured was magic that hurt pretty bad. Yet Gemma hadn't seen any such magic when Cináed fought. Actually, all she'd seen with him was brute strength that made her giddy watching him.

Gemma focused and managed to see the ball of magic coming toward her right before it slammed into her. She jumped out of the way as Cináed let out a bellow that turned into a roar so loud she dropped to her knees and covered her ears.

Then it dawned on her who had made that sound. She lowered her hands and turned her head to see a dragon. Her mouth fell open when she saw the bluish-white sheen she recognized all too well. Moonstone was one of her favorite gems.

She couldn't take her eyes off the thick body and tail of the dragon, er Cináed. The nearly colorless scales appeared metallic and picked up various colors near them. And his wings were so extraordinary that she wanted to touch them.

The size of him was enough to give anyone pause, but if that didn't do it then the long claws, spike on the end of the tail, and the long teeth whenever he opened his mouth surely would.

His big head shifted and she saw his eyes the color of spun gold meet hers. Without thinking, Gemma rushed to him, coming to stand between his front legs. He then flapped his wings toward Usaeil. It created such a wind gust that she fought to remain on her feet.

But Cináed wasn't nearly done.

She heard his intake of breath. Out of the corner of her eye she saw something bright for just a moment. Usaeil's eyes widened as he breathed fire.

Sweat ran down Gemma's face from the heat of the fire. She had never felt anything so hot in her life and she was safely sheltered from it. She couldn't imagine being in it. But at least Usaeil was gone.

Gemma leaned against Cináed's leg. She smiled at the warmth of the scales before she rested her head against him. Cináed issued a curious noise that almost sounded like a purr.

When the smoke cleared, she expected to see ash or whatever was left of Usaeil's body, but there was nothing but charred earth.

Cináed tensed. Gemma lifted her head and let her gaze scan the area, looking for Usaeil. The queen had promised to end her life, and Gemma knew the Fae wouldn't give up so easily.

"You didn't really think to get me with dragon fire, did you?"

Cináed roared at the sound of Usaeil's voice. He turned, but it wasn't in time. Gemma heard the Fae say something. The next instant Cináed was in human form, naked, with death in his gray eyes as he stared at Usaeil.

He pulled back his hands as if gathering his magic, but Usaeil simply smiled and said something else Gemma didn't understand. Cináed crumpled to the ground.

Gemma gaped at him in shock. What had the queen said to cause such a reaction from Cináed? She opened her lips to scream for Merrill, but no words came out.

"Now. Where were we?" Usaeil asked from beside her.

She tried to run, but the queen grabbed her by the neck and threw her to the ground.

Chapter Twenty-two

"Wake up!"

Merrill's voice in Cináed's head bellowed again and again until he stirred. Then came the feeling that Gemma was in danger. The rain pelted his face as he opened his eyes to find Usaeil standing over Gemma with her hands around his woman's neck.

"Keep hidden for now," he told Merrill.

"The Clacher line has lived long enough," Usaeil said as she straddled Gemma. "It was by my mercy alone that you had as many years as you did."

Gemma lifted her knee, slamming it into the queen's back to break her hold, but it did no good. Cináed saw her struggling to get breath into her lungs. He tried to roll over, but he couldn't. That's when he felt it—the magic.

It wasn't regular Fae magic. This was something else entirely. Something that felt...wrong.

His gaze snapped to Usaeil's face. They believed she was just a part of the Others, but Cináed was beginning to think she played a much bigger role.

But that could be discussed later. Right now he had to get to Gemma, because there was no way Usaeil was going to take his mate from him.

Cináed thrashed against the invisible bonds holding him. Even as the magic tightened around him, cutting into his skin like wires, he fought. The pain only made him more determined to get free and reach Gemma.

Because she was all that mattered.

Usaeil's laughter caught his attention. He looked at the Queen of the Light to find her gaze on him, her smile wide.

"Look at him," Usaeil bade Gemma. "Look how he lies there unable to get to you. Dragon Kings claim to be the strongest creatures of this realm. That's a lie."

Cináed peeled back his lips, baring his teeth. He didn't care how much Con wanted to attack Usaeil, if Cináed got a chance, he was going to rip out her black heart.

"You're...jealous." Gemma's voice was strained, but her words were clear. As was the fury in her pale blue eyes.

Usaeil's head cocked to the side as her attention swung back to Gemma. "What are you trying to say?"

To Cináed's relief, the queen loosened her hold on Gemma's neck. He redoubled his efforts against Usaeil's magic. He wanted to shift, but she had used a spell that prevented that for the time being.

He gritted his teeth and used his strength. It got him through most of the invisible bindings. The last bit, he used his magic to sever.

"Tell me," Usaeil ordered Gemma.

Gemma smiled and removed her hands from the queen. To Cináed's shock, Gemma rested her arms along the wet ground as her body went slack.

"You want what the Kings have," Gemma said. "Their power. Their respect. You envy them."

Usaeil was so focused on Gemma that she never saw Cináed get to his feet.

The queen snorted derisively. "Envy them? They hide and cower while the Fae thrive. They are the ones who envy me."

"And Con?" Gemma asked.

Usaeil's gaze narrowed. "Don't talk about what you don't know."

"I know he doesn't want you."

Cináed smiled. Leave it to his woman to be spunky and tell it to the queen as only she could.

"You know nothing!" Usaeil shouted.

Gemma's lips curved into a smile. "I know that if a King finds someone, then he will do whatever it takes to be with her. Con isn't doing that for you."

"He needs to see how good we are together."

"Or maybe you need to realize that he was never yours to have."

Malice contorted Usaeil's face as she tightened her fingers on Gemma's throat again. Cináed slammed his magic into the queen, sending her rolling to the side. She screeched the moment she landed in a puddle.

Cináed rushed to Gemma and yanked her to her feet. Their gazes met and Gemma gave him a nod to let him know she was okay. Then he pushed her behind him.

Usaeil climbed to her feet, her eyes locked on them. "You can't stop me from killing her. Today, tomorrow, or next year, I will exact my retribution."

"You had your chance," Cináed told her. "You lost it."

"Merrill. Get ready," he told his friend.

Usaeil stalked toward them. Cináed readied his magic as he saw Merrill, in dragon form, rise from the waters behind the queen. But before Cináed could trap the queen, Gemma walked around him, her hand out.

"Gemma!" he yelled.

But she ignored him as she collided with Usaeil's chest. Cináed rushed to her.

"I know what you are," Gemma told the queen. "I know what you've done."

Usaeil tried to throw off Gemma's hand, but it didn't budge. Cináed's eyes bulged. His mate didn't have any magic, nor did he feel any from her then, so he wasn't sure how she was able to contain the Queen of the Light.

"My ancestors told me about you," Gemma continued.

Usaeil's face went slack.

Gemma smiled, nodding, as she dropped her arm to her side. "Exactly. Your retribution is coming. At long last."

The queen jerked back and took several steps away. "You're bluffing."

"Am I?" Gemma asked.

Without another word, Usaeil teleported away.

"What the bloody hell just happened?" Cináed asked.

Gemma stared to turn to face him, but she caught sight of Merrill and paused to look at him. With a wave in his direction, she faced Cináed. Without saying anything, she took his hand and led him to the house.

It wasn't long after they entered that Merrill strode inside fully clothed. They exchanged looks, both confused about what they'd seen.

Gemma wrung out her hair while Cináed used magic to cover his nakedness. She looked at ease, as if she had found her way through the tangle of the past.

"My father bought this isle not just because it was private, but also because many of my ancestors had lived on it as well. It was those ancestors who stood beside me today."

Cináed watched her carefully to make sure it wasn't some trick of Usaeil's magic.

Gemma laughed softly and walked to him. "I'm all right. I promise. Other than a sore throat and back, Usaeil didn't hurt me."

"Explain the ancestors comment," Merrill urged.

She shrugged. "There isn't much to say. I felt them with me before Usaeil arrived. They tried to talk to me while she was here, but I didn't realize what was happening. It wasn't until she was choking me and I was about to pass out that I heard them clearly."

"What did they say?" Cináed asked.

"Quite a lot actually. I'll get to that in a second."

Cináed pulled her close, needing to hold her. "And the way she wasn't able to swat your hand away."

Gemma ducked her head, but there was a smile when she looked back at him. "You kept telling me I was a Clacher. My ancestors told me the same thing."

"Clachers can sense Druids," Merrill said.

She nodded, glancing his way. "Exactly. I sensed Druid magic mixed in with Usaeil's."

"I'll be damned," Cináed said, thinking back to how odd the queen's magic felt. "You're right. It was Druid and Fae magic that she hit me with."

Gemma lifted one shoulder. "Once I heard my ancestors, I knew I had to touch her. Somehow, that hindered the Druid magic she had taken."

"You told her you knew what she had done."

"The Druid magic she has she took from another by killing them."

Merrill ran a hand through his wet hair. "Why does that no' surprise me?"

"And her retribution?" Cináed asked.

Gemma gave a shake of her head. "I don't know. The ancestors told me to say that."

"Rhi," Merrill said. "It has to be."

Cináed was thinking the same thing. There was a lot to share with the others when they returned to Dreagan.

Merrill blew out a breath. "What now?"

"I have my answers," Gemma said.

Cináed smoothed back a wet lock that had escaped her ponytail. "I'm sorry."

"Knowing helps." The sadness gave way to determination. "I also found who I am. I took the Clacher name because I found it, or so I thought. I believe my ancestors were with me that night my family died. I think they helped me know to keep away from Usaeil and where to hide. I also think they led me to the Clacher name. I carry it proudly. No longer will I hide."

He bowed his head and pressed his lips against her. He'd always seen the strength within her. Now she wore it like armor instead of hiding it.

"What about Usaeil coming for you later?" Merrill asked.

That had been Cináed's next question.

Gemma shrugged. "I may not be able to do magic like other Druids, but I come from a long line of them. The ancestors told me that one of the Clacher abilities that made them so great at regulating Druids is that we can dampen their magic so they can't use it."

"Holy fuck," Merrill said, smiling.

Cináed laughed and kissed her forehead. "I knew you were special."

Gemma raised her face to him. "Thank you for helping me get through this."

"You didna need me."

"Yes, I did. More than you'll ever know."

His heart swelled with pride and love. This woman was astonishing, and he couldn't believe she was in his arms.

"What now?" she asked.

He glanced toward Merrill to find that his friend had quietly slipped out to leave them alone. "Well, that's up to you."

"You did promise me some time alone," she said with a grin.

"And you'll get it. As much as you want, any time you want it."

She gave a nod. "But we need to go to Dreagan first."

"Aye, we do. Con needs to know what transpired here."

"I understand."

Cináed rubbed his hands up and down her back. "It's the after part that's up to you. I've fallen hard for you, Gemma. I know you've been on your own for a long time, and I'll give you whatever space you need.

All I ask is that you remain in my life."

"I don't want any space. I just want you."

Elation ran through him. "I doona want to scare you, but I want you to know that I love you."

"That's a good thing since I love you as well."

Cináed lifted her in his arms as he hugged her tight. "Ah, lass, you've made me so happy."

"Not nearly as happy as you've made me." She pulled back to cup his face in her hands. "I'm yours, Cináed. For as long as you want me."

"That's forever, love."

"Then forever it is."

Epilogue

Gemma wasn't sure she would ever learn everyone's name at Dreagan, but she couldn't wait to try. No longer was she the antisocial person from before. She was a new woman.

Welcoming didn't even begin to describe how everyone made her feel. She would even go so far as to say that Con was pleased to have her among them. Though she hated to admit she'd been tongue-tied when they met. Cináed hadn't warned her she was about to meet the King of Dragon Kings.

"Happy, love?" Cináed asked as he tightened his arms around her.

She nodded her head that lay on his chest. They'd returned to the cottage on Skye for a few days to themselves. And just as he'd promised, they hadn't left the bed. "Immensely. You?"

"More than you could possibly imagine."

"I can't wait to spend more time with Henry and Esther. Do you really think we're related?"

He chuckled. "I do believe you are."

"I have family," she said and smiled.

"Don't forget everyone at Dreagan."

She didn't reply because she wasn't sure how to. They had professed their love to each other, but she didn't know what that entailed, and she hadn't wanted to bring it up.

"Gemma?" he pressed as he shifted her so that she looked up at him. "You do understand those at Dreagan are family, right?"

"Yes." Though it came out a bit hastily.

He frowned but the lines softened as he rolled her onto her back. "Just so we're clear, I want you as my mate, Gemma Clacher. You tell me when you're ready to make it official, and I'll see it done."

She stared into his gray eyes, undone by the love and desire he'd shown her. "I've been yours, Cináed. I'll always be yours."

"Ah, lass," he murmured before he kissed her.

They were interrupted by a knock at the door. He leaned back and said, "You better get that."

Gemma frowned, but wrapped a sheet around her as she went to the door. She opened it and found a large box sitting there wrapped in a big bow. She glanced at Cináed to find him watching her as he lay propped up on an elbow.

"Open it," he bade.

She squatted down, biting her lip. She couldn't remember the last time anyone had given her a gift. Excitement and nervousness rushed through her as she lifted shaking hands to the lid.

The moment she removed the lid, a puppy rose up on its hind legs, using the side of the box for its front paws, and licked her face.

"Oh, my God," she exclaimed as she gathered the squirming puppy in her arms.

Cináed was beside her then. "We can still adopt as many senior dogs as you want, but I really wanted to get you a puppy."

"I love him. Or her," she said laughing as the puppy continued to lick her while also trying to get to Cináed. "And I love you."

He wrapped his arms around her as they stood holding the puppy. The road before them wasn't going to be smooth—she did have the Queen of the Light as an enemy—but she had Cináed. And that was all she needed.

* * * *

It was a setback. One Usaeil hadn't counted on. She thought she knew everything about the Clachers, but Gemma had surprised her.

She looked down at her hands. The mortal had simply touched her and prevented her magic from working. How had she done it? More importantly, could Gemma do it again? Not to mention Gemma was a Dragon King mate, which made things even trickier.

Usaeil paced the room, her mind working through her plans. She was going to have to change a few things around. She halted and grinned. Although that might not be a bad thing. She knew Con and the Dragon Kings well enough to know what their next step would be.

Same with Rhi.

Oh, yes. They'd never see what she had coming for them.

* * * *

Also from 1001 Dark Nights and Donna Grant, discover Dragon Night, Dragon King, Dragon Fever, and Dragon Burn.

Sign up for the 1001 Dark Nights Newsletter
and be entered to win a Tiffany Key necklace.

There's a contest every month!

Go to www.1001DarkNights.com to subscribe.

As a bonus, all subscribers can download
FIVE FREE exclusive books!

Discover 1001 Dark Nights Collection Six

Go to www.1001DarkNights.com for more information.

DRAGON CLAIMED by Donna Grant
A Dark Kings Novella

ASHES TO INK by Carrie Ann Ryan
A Montgomery Ink: Colorado Springs Novella

ENSNARED by Elisabeth Naughton
An Eternal Guardians Novella

EVERMORE by Corinne Michaels
A Salvation Series Novella

VENGEANCE by Rebecca Zanetti
A Dark Protectors/Rebels Novella

ELI'S TRIUMPH by Joanna Wylde
A Reapers MC Novella

CIPHER by Larissa Ione
A Demonica Underworld Novella

RESCUING MACIE by Susan Stoker
A Delta Force Heroes Novella

ENCHANTED by Lexi Blake
A Masters and Mercenaries Novella

TAKE THE BRIDE by Carly Phillips
A Knight Brothers Novella

INDULGE ME by J. Kenner
A Stark Ever After Novella

THE KING by Jennifer L. Armentrout
A Wicked Novella

QUIET MAN by Kristen Ashley
A Dream Man Novella

ABANDON by Rachel Van Dyken
A Seaside Pictures Novella

THE OPEN DOOR by Laurelin Paige
A Found Duet Novella

CLOSER by Kylie Scott
A Stage Dive Novella

SOMETHING JUST LIKE THIS by Jennifer Probst
A Stay Novella

BLOOD NIGHT by Heather Graham
A Krewe of Hunters Novella

TWIST OF FATE by Jill Shalvis
A Heartbreaker Bay Novella

MORE THAN PLEASURE YOU by Shayla Black
A More Than Words Novella

WONDER WITH ME by Kristen Proby
A With Me In Seattle Novella

THE DARKEST ASSASSIN by Gena Showalter
A Lords of the Underworld Novella

Discover 1001 Dark Nights

Go to www.1001DarkNights.com for more information.

FOREVER WICKED by Shayla Black
CRIMSON TWILIGHT by Heather Graham
CAPTURED IN SURRENDER by Liliana Hart
SILENT BITE: A SCANGUARDS WEDDING by Tina Folsom
DUNGEON GAMES by Lexi Blake
AZAGOTH by Larissa Ione
NEED YOU NOW by Lisa Renee Jones
SHOW ME, BABY by Cherise Sinclair
ROPED IN by Lorelei James
TEMPTED BY MIDNIGHT by Lara Adrian
THE FLAME by Christopher Rice
CARESS OF DARKNESS by Julie Kenner
WICKED WOLF by Carrie Ann Ryan
WHEN IRISH EYES ARE HAUNTING by Heather Graham
EASY WITH YOU by Kristen Proby
MASTER OF FREEDOM by Cherise Sinclair
CARESS OF PLEASURE by Julie Kenner
ADORED by Lexi Blake
HADES by Larissa Ione
RAVAGED by Elisabeth Naughton
DREAM OF YOU by Jennifer L. Armentrout
STRIPPED DOWN by Lorelei James
RAGE/KILLIAN by Alexandra Ivy/Laura Wright
DRAGON KING by Donna Grant
PURE WICKED by Shayla Black
HARD AS STEEL by Laura Kaye
STROKE OF MIDNIGHT by Lara Adrian
ALL HALLOWS EVE by Heather Graham
KISS THE FLAME by Christopher Rice
DARING HER LOVE by Melissa Foster
TEASED by Rebecca Zanetti
THE PROMISE OF SURRENDER by Liliana Hart
HIDDEN INK by Carrie Ann Ryan
BLOOD ON THE BAYOU by Heather Graham
SEARCHING FOR MINE by Jennifer Probst
DANCE OF DESIRE by Christopher Rice

ROUGH RHYTHM by Tessa Bailey
DEVOTED by Lexi Blake
Z by Larissa Ione
FALLING UNDER YOU by Laurelin Paige
EASY FOR KEEPS by Kristen Proby
UNCHAINED by Elisabeth Naughton
HARD TO SERVE by Laura Kaye
DRAGON FEVER by Donna Grant
KAYDEN/SIMON by Alexandra Ivy/Laura Wright
STRUNG UP by Lorelei James
MIDNIGHT UNTAMED by Lara Adrian
TRICKED by Rebecca Zanetti
DIRTY WICKED by Shayla Black
THE ONLY ONE by Lauren Blakely
SWEET SURRENDER by Liliana Hart
ROCK CHICK REAWAKENING by Kristen Ashley
ADORING INK by Carrie Ann Ryan
SWEET RIVALRY by K. Bromberg
SHADE'S LADY by Joanna Wylde
RAZR by Larissa Ione
ARRANGED by Lexi Blake
TANGLED by Rebecca Zanetti
HOLD ME by J. Kenner
SOMEHOW, SOME WAY by Jennifer Probst
TOO CLOSE TO CALL by Tessa Bailey
HUNTED by Elisabeth Naughton
EYES ON YOU by Laura Kaye
BLADE by Alexandra Ivy/Laura Wright
DRAGON BURN by Donna Grant
TRIPPED OUT by Lorelei James
STUD FINDER by Lauren Blakely
MIDNIGHT UNLEASHED by Lara Adrian
HALLOW BE THE HAUNT by Heather Graham
DIRTY FILTHY FIX by Laurelin Paige
THE BED MATE by Kendall Ryan
NIGHT GAMES by CD Reiss
NO RESERVATIONS by Kristen Proby
DAWN OF SURRENDER by Liliana Hart
BLAZE ERUPTING by Rebecca Zanetti

ROUGH RIDE by Kristen Ashley
HAWKYN by Larissa Ione
RIDE DIRTY by Laura Kaye
ROME'S CHANCE by Joanna Wylde
THE MARRIAGE ARRANGEMENT by Jennifer Probst
SURRENDER by Elisabeth Naughton
INKED NIGHTS by Carrie Ann Ryan
ENVY by Rachel Van Dyken
PROTECTED by Lexi Blake
THE PRINCE by Jennifer L. Armentrout
PLEASE ME by J. Kenner
WOUND TIGHT by Lorelei James
STRONG by Kylie Scott
DRAGON NIGHT by Donna Grant
TEMPTING BROOKE by Kristen Proby
HAUNTED BE THE HOLIDAYS by Heather Graham
CONTROL by K. Bromberg
HUNKY HEARTBREAKER by Kendall Ryan
THE DARKEST CAPTIVE by Gena Showalter

Also from 1001 Dark Nights:

TAME ME by J. Kenner
THE SURRENDER GATE By Christopher Rice
SERVICING THE TARGET By Cherise Sinclair
TEMPT ME by J. Kenner

About Donna Grant

New York Times and USA Today bestselling author Donna Grant has been praised for her "totally addictive" and "unique and sensual" stories. She's the author of more than eighty novels spanning multiple genres of romance. Her latest acclaimed series, Dark Kings, features dragons, the Fae, and immortal Highlanders who are dark, dangerous, and irresistible.

She lives with her two children, one dog, and four cats in Texas.

For more information about Donna, visit her website at www.DonnaGrant.com or www.MotherofDragonsBooks.com.

Discover More Donna Grant

Dragon Night
A Dark Kings Novella
By Donna Grant

Governed by honor and ruled by desire

There has never been a hunt that Dorian has lost. With his sights sent on a relic the Dragon Kings need to battle an ancient foe, he won't let anything stand in his way – especially not the beautiful owner. Alexandra is smart and cautious. Yet the attraction between them is impossible to deny – or ignore. But is it a road Dorian dares to travel down again?

With her vast family fortune, Alexandra Sheridan is never without suitors. No one is more surprised than she when the charming, devilish Scotsman snags her attention. But the secrets Dorian holds is like a wall between them until one fateful night when he shares everything. In his arms she finds passion like no other – and a love that will transcend time. But can she give her heart to a dragon??

* * * *

Dragon Burn
A Dark Kings Novella
By Donna Grant

In this scorching Dark Kings novella, *New York Times* bestselling author Donna Grant brings together a determined Dragon King used to getting what he wants and an Ice Queen who thaws for no one.

Marked by passion

A promise made eons ago sends Sebastian to Italy on the hunt to find an enemy. His quarry proves difficult to locate, but there is someone who can point him in the right direction – a woman as frigid as the north. Using every seductive skill he's acquired over his immortal life, his seduction begins. Until he discovers that the passion he stirs within her makes him burn for more…

Gianna Santini has one love in her life — work. A disastrous failed marriage was evidence enough to realize she was better off on her own. That is until a handsome Scot strolled into her life and literally swept her off her feet. She is unprepared for the blazing passion between them or the truth he exposes. But as her world begins to unravel, she realizes the only one she can depend on is the very one destroying everything - a Dragon King.

* * * *

Dragon Fever
A Dark Kings Novella
By Donna Grant

A yearning that won't be denied

Rachel Marek is a journalist with a plan. She intends to expose the truth about dragons to the world — and her target is within sight. Nothing matters but getting the truth, especially not the ruggedly handsome, roguishly thrilling Highlander who oozes danger and charm. And when she finds the truth that shatters her faith, she'll have to trust her heart to the very man who can crush it…

A legend in the flesh

Suave, dashing Asher is more than just a man. He's a Dragon King — a being who has roamed this planet since the beginning of time. With everything on the line, Asher must choose to trust an enemy in the form of an all too alluring woman whose tenacity and passion captivate him. Together, Asher and Rachel must fight for their lives — and their love — before an old enemy destroys them both…

* * * *

Dragon King
A Dark Kings Novella
By Donna Grant

A Woman On A Mission

Grace Clark has always done things safe. She's never colored outside of the law, but she has a book due and has found the perfect spot to break through her writer's block. Or so she thinks. Right up until Arian suddenly appears and tries to force her away from the mountain. Unaware of the war she just stumbled into, Grace doesn't just discover the perfect place to write, she finds Arian - the most gorgeous, enticing, mysterious man she's ever met.

A King With a Purpose

Arian is a Dragon King who has slept away centuries in his cave. Recently woken, he's about to leave his mountain to join his brethren in a war when he's alerted that someone has crossed onto Dreagan. He's ready to fight...until he sees the woman. She's innocent and mortal - and she sets his blood aflame. He recognizes the danger approaching her just as the dragon within him demands he claim her for his own...

Ignite

By Donna Grant
Dark Kings 15
Coming April 30, 2019

Things weren't going good, and they didn't look to be improving any time soon.

V ran a hand down his face wearily. All he wanted was to go to his mountain and figure out why his sword wouldn't work. But he couldn't. If he did, every Dragon King at Dreagan would know something was wrong.

Eons after having his sword stolen and then hidden from him, it was now back in his grasp. But it did no good. Every King was counting on him to use it in order to check on the dragons.

He paced his room inside the manor, wondering if it was somehow his fault that his weapon wouldn't respond to him anymore. Had he done something to...? That couldn't be it. The sword was his, part of him. All Dragons Kings had a sword that only they could use.

So if it wasn't him, then what was it? What kept him from being able to use his sword to check on the dragons? Ever since the Kings forced the dragons to leave during the war with the humans, they had no idea if their clans were alive or not. The Kings didn't even know where the dragons were.

The dragon bridge was manifested from the combined magic of all the Kings, and it was the one and only time they had ever used such a bridge.

V couldn't stay in his chamber any more. He stalked from his room and made his way downstairs. As he walked across the vast expanse of Dreagan – staying far from the Visitor's Center at the distillery where people lined up to take tours – he was glad he didn't run into any of his brethren.

Only Cináed knew about his conundrum. If this continued, V would have no choice but to tell the rest of the Kings. After all he and Roman gone through in Iceland just to find his stolen sword, it wasn't right that he couldn't make it work properly.

V kept walking. He didn't care were he went. He just needed to burn off some of the anger and anxiety that churned like a raging storm within him. His first choice would be shifting into his true form and taking to the skies, but that wasn't something they could do during the day. The fact they were hiding from the humans prevented that.

V could use his power. Every Dragon King was granted a special type of magic. For him, it was being able to disguise his dragon form when he shifted. He was so tempted to do that, but he didn't. It wouldn't be fair for him to take to the skies while others could not.

He had no idea how much time passed before he found himself walking along a paved road. V paused and looked up to get his bearings. He was no longer on Dreagan, and with their land encompassing sixty thousand acres that meant he had walked quite a ways.

V heard the roar of an approaching engine. He grimaced when he recognized the unmistakable sound of the Maseratti GranTurismo MC Stradale that belonged to none other than Constantine, King of Dragon Kings.

He watched as the bright blue sports car came into view. And just as expected, Con slowed when he spotted V. The Dragon Kings were the most powerful of beings on the realm, but even they had someone to answer to. That someone was Constantine.

Con rolled down his window, his black eyes locking on V's face. He was attired in his usual – a suit, starched shirt, gold dragon head cufflinks, and no tie. "Everything all right?" he asked.

V nodded. "Just walking."

A blond brow shot up on Con's forehead. "Toward the village?"

"I needed to stretch my legs."

"And you couldn't do that on Dreagan? Or was it that you didn't want to run into any Kings?"

V blew out a breath and looked over the top of the car to the opposite side of the road where sheep grazed on the steep hills.

"I see," Con said after a moment. "You know you can talk to me about whatever is troubling you."

"I know." V met Con's black gaze. "I just need some time. Finally having my sword back after so many millions of years without it is taking some getting used to."

Con blinked, his expression devoid of any emotion, but V knew him well enough to know that Con was trying to discover what it was V hid. It was one of the many reasons Con was King of Kings.

"You know where to find me," Con replied.

V gave a nod. Con stared at him a moment longer before he drove off. The last thing anyone at Dreagan needed was the knowledge that something was wrong with his sword. With all he and Roman had discovered in the mountain on Iceland in regards to the Others, there was much the Kings had to do.

The Others.

The mere thought of them made V want to retaliate. The mysterious group was a mix of good and evil Druids as well as Dark and Light Fae. Why such an alliance would come together still confused to the Kings.

Worse, the Others seemed to be after the Dragon Kings. And they had waited thousands of years before taking action. Though no one knew why the Others had been so patient.

Or what they were after.

V waited until he saw the taillights of Con's car disappear over a hill before he turned and resumed his walk. He couldn't think about the Others right now. He had to focus on his sword. Yet, the two were connected.

It was the Others who initially tried to get his sword. Fortunately, a group of humans that V once protected discovered the Others' plan. The humans used their skills to steal the weapon from V and hide it before the Others could lay claim to it.

He wished the gypsies would have told him their plan, but he knew he wouldn't have listened to them had they tried. He would've told them he could take care of things himself. The truth, however, was that he would've underestimated the Others. And the gypsies had not.

It was the Others who spelled V so he lost his memories about when and how his sword was stolen. But he now had them returned. His memories gave him little insight into the group, however. What it did show him was the lengths some mortals would go to in order to help the Dragon Kings.

That was in direct opposition to what the majority of humans had done to the Kings, which began the war between them. V still couldn't believe that the Dragon Kings, the strongest, greatest beings on the realm, had given up *everything* to the mortals.

That was a road he didn't need to wander down. His mind returned to the Others. Despite the attempt by the gypsies, the Others found the man who had taken his sword. The gypsies made sure that the Others couldn't touch it. Instead, the nefarious group put other traps in place throughout the mountain in Iceland to hinder anyone trying to retrieve the weapon.

It was through great difficulty and the help of friends that V and Roman were able to escape the mountain not only with their lives, but with the sword as well.

This wasn't the first time the Others had set ruses and deceptions for the Kings. Perhaps it was because of the tricks the Others used that made V apprehensive. First, it was the wooden dragon carved as a replica of Con. One touch to that figurine caused chaos to erupt.

There was also the incident in New York with the black dagger and a fellow King, Dorian.

And now this.

At least, those were the only ones he knew of. There could be more. That in itself made his worry double.

It had taken V all of his considerable magic and strength to bust through the magic woven through his memories from the Others. For millions of years, he hadn't known anyone touched his memories. But now he knew what to look for.

His mind was clean of any enchantment from the Others, but he hadn't checked his sword yet. In fact, he hadn't held it since attempting to use it after returning to Dreagan.

For eons, he'd lived with the knowledge that he'd failed as a King because mortals had stolen his sword. While he now knew the truth, it didn't help him feel any better.

He was a Dragon King. No one should have been able to get to him through magic. No one. But they did.

With tragic results.

If he'd kept a hold of his sword, he could have checked on the dragons several times. And called them home.

V looked up and found himself standing in front of the medical clinic. Sophie, who was mated to another King, Darius, ran it. Many of the Kings hadn't been sure how Sophie could continue to work as a doctor and keep the secrets of Dreagan, but so far she'd done wonders.

She wouldn't be able to do that forever though. As a mate, she was given the gift of immortality. Sophie had a few more years before others began to notice that she didn't age. Then she would have to close the practice for a few generations before she could once more open it back up.

V's gaze swung to the parking lot as he heard the squeal of tires as a white Mini with black racing stripes pulled to a stop. He sidestepped behind a tree and watched as Claire got out of her car. V couldn't understand how she drove so fast and didn't worry about being killed. He gave her credit for being an expert driver, but mortals only had one life. He really wished she would slow down.

Her blonde locks were haphazardly pulled back into what he had heard Sophie describe as a messy bun — whatever that was. He didn't care what it was called. He just knew that he liked it on Claire. What he liked more was when she left her locks free to fall down her back.

She was always changing her look. Some days she had on vivid makeup with her long hair styled in various ways. Other days she had on very little makeup and a messy bun.

He liked them all.

The few times he happened to be near when Claire arrived at the clinic she would make her way into the office singing from whatever had been blaring on her car radio, but today she was subdued. Her oval face was pensive, as if she were deep in thought.

She adjusted the big black bag she carried on her shoulder before she pulled out her mobile. The moment she looked at the screen, she stopped. A second later, a smile broke out over her face.

V found himself grinning in response because her smile — even when not directed at him — was infectious. He didn't know what it was about the blonde beauty that first captured his attention and hadn't let go since.

His vantage point gave him perfect access to her face. Whatever was on the phone lit up her face. He'd seen the mated Kings do that to their women. V wondered if he would ever cause someone to smile like that.

The majority of his life after the war with the humans had been spent sleeping in his mountain. He hadn't had time to think of anything more than reclaiming his stolen sword. Now...now, all around him were those who had something to occupy them in regards to Dreagan.

Then there were those who had found love.

It was difficult to be around so many who were happy. Those like Vaughn, who was a solicitor for Dreagan, who found their place in the human world. Then there were the pairs who were always together, always sharing secret words and looks. And touches.

Eons of time spent alone crushed V under the weight of it all. He thought sex would help. And it had. For a short while. Then that haunting ache filled his chest again.

He wasn't stupid. He knew exactly what it was. Loneliness. He was surrounded by his brethren, but felt utterly, completely alone.

V drew in a deep breath and watched Claire's pace quicken as she hurried into the clinic. He shifted around the tree to continue to observe her, catching one last look before she walked through the door, disappearing into the building.

He'd spent a lot of time at the clinic lately helping out when it was needed. Most of the Kings did from time to time. Sophie was part of the family, and as such, they were always there for whatever she needed.

Not that Darius couldn't handle things himself, but sometimes it was just an excuse to be together. Just as everyone not only went to Laith's pub, but also helped out there as well. The Dragon King had owned the pub for hundreds of years, legally passing it down to himself and disappearing for decades at a time.

Who knew how long such things would work. The people of the village near Dreagan seemed happy. Then again, so had the mortals before the war began.

"She's pretty, is she no'?"

V closed his eyes at the sound of Darius's voice. He should've heard Darius approach, and he would have had he not been so engrossed in Claire.

He opened his eyes and turned to face his friend. He could try to lie, but there was no point. "Aye. She certainly is."

"Sophie and Claire are very close," Darius stated.

V quirked a brow. "I'm aware of that."

"I know you've picked up Rhys's habits of a different woman every night —"

V was affronted by the charge. "It's no' every night."

"Somehow, despite everything that happened in Edinburgh to her and Sophie, Claire doesna know about us."

V crossed his arms over his chest. He didn't know the entire story about how Claire and Sophie were taken by the Dark Fae, but he knew that it had been a close call for both women. "Are you sure she doesna?"

Darius glanced at the building. "She would've said something to Sophie if she did. You're welcome at the clinic anytime, but Claire is like a sister to Sophie."

"You want me to keep away from her." And somehow, that hurt V more than he'd expected.

"If you think she could be your mate, then I'll no' stand in your way."

"I didna say that."

Darius nodded slowly. "I just doona want Claire hurt."

V squared his shoulders. "I'm well aware that she is off limits."

Darius gave a nod of appreciation. "Thank you. Since you're here, I could really use your help moving some more boxes. I never knew so much was needed to run a medical clinic."

V was slow to follow Darius. While he understood his friend's caution, nonetheless, he was hurt by it. More than that, he wondered at the lie he'd told about Claire. And the consequences of not admitting what he'd known in his heart for some time now.

On behalf of 1001 Dark Nights,
Liz Berry and M.J. Rose would like to thank ~

Steve Berry
Doug Scofield
Kim Guidroz
Jillian Stein
InkSlinger PR
Dan Slater
Asha Hossain
Chris Graham
Fedora Chen
Kasi Alexander
Jessica Johns
Dylan Stockton
Richard Blake
and Simon Lipskar

Made in the USA
Middletown, DE
28 November 2023

43803820R00104